ANUNNAKI

ANUNNAKI

JOSE LUIS ROBLEDO

ARCHWAY
PUBLISHING

Archway Publishing books may be ordered through booksellers or by contacting:

Archway Publishing
1663 Liberty Drive
Bloomington, IN 47403
www.archwaypublishing.com
844-669-3957

ISBN: 978-1-6657-6449-0 (sc)
ISBN: 978-1-6657-6451-3 (hc)
ISBN: 978-1-6657-6450-6 (e)

Library of Congress Control Number: 2024916958

Print information available on the last page.

Archway Publishing rev. date: 09/27/2024

Disclaimer

This book is a work of fiction inspired by true events. While elements of the story are based on real-life occurrences, characters, and historical events, the overall narrative and specific details have been fictionalized for dramatic effect and storytelling purposes.

The author has taken creative liberties to weave together a compelling and engaging story, but readers should be aware that certain aspects, dialogues, and scenes may have been altered, exaggerated, or entirely imagined to enhance the reading experience.

While efforts have been made to ensure the accuracy and authenticity of the events portrayed in this book, it is important to note that the primary aim is to entertain rather than provide a factual account. The author encourages readers to independently explore the real historical events that inspired this work for a more comprehensive understanding.

Furthermore, any resemblance to actual persons, living or dead, is purely coincidental. Names, character traits, and physical descriptions used in this book are the product of the author's imagination and are not intended to represent or accurately reflect real individuals.

The intention of this book is to capture the essence of the true events, from which it draws inspiration, and to offer readers an immersive and captivating fictional story set against a backdrop of real historical context.

Readers should approach this book with the understanding that it is a blend of fact and fiction and allow themselves to be entertained by the narrative while keeping in mind that certain liberties have been taken for storytelling purposes.

CONTENTS

I dedicate this book to my partner, Tong, to my daughters, Veronica, Dana, Sandra, Stephanie, and Paula, who inspired and encouraged me to write this book, and to all my family members, who have been very supportive of me.

ACKNOWLEDGMENTS

I want to thank Wikipedia for all the wonderful articles available online, which makes research very efficient. Thank you to Google Chrome for making it very easy to search for articles I needed for research. Thank you to all the authors of books and articles online and historians for their incredibly good work, which is available to the public. Thank you to the Facebook groups such as "The Anunnaki," "Giorgio Tsoukalos," and "Erich von Daniken Ancient Aliens," where so many members inspired me with their views on topics covered in my book. Thank you to everyone who helped me in one way or another.

PROLOGUE

....

In the dimly lit chambers of the holy Inquisition, whispers of conspiracy echoed against stone walls stained with history. In the kingdom of Castile, Toledo, it was the fifteenth century—a time when fear ruled hearts, and the power of the Church was absolute. Amidst this atmosphere of uncertainty and suspicion, an ancient secret society known only as One World Order (OWO) emerged. Its tendrils creeped into the highest echelons of religious authority. Its agenda was whispered in hushed tones among the most trusted confidants of the Inquisition. These whispers spoke of a diabolical pact to wield not only temporal but supernatural control over humankind. Its sinister plots were said to include dark rituals invoking ancient entities, which were all aimed at bending the will of humanity to its malevolent desires.

As rumors grew louder, dissent began to brew within the ranks of the faithful. Some among the clergy dared to voice their suspicions and pointed accusatory fingers at the Inquisition itself, claiming it had been infiltrated and overtaken by this demonic secret society. These voices of dissent were labeled heretics and were accused of consorting with the very darkness they claimed to expose.

Among the accused was Father Ignatius, a devout priest known for his unwavering faith and staunch defense of the Church's teachings. Yet his outspoken nature, unwavering belief in righteousness, and warning to the church leaders made him a target for those who sought to silence any challenge to their authority. One fateful night, masked figures clad in black seized Father Ignatius from his chambers and accused him of spreading lies and conspiracies against the Inquisition.

Dragged before a tribunal of judges, who were shrouded in shadow, Father Ignatius stood firm. His face was defiant despite the fear that gnawed at his soul. The charges against him were read aloud; each word dripped with venomous accusation. He was branded a heretic and servant of darkness masquerading as a shepherd of light.

The trial was a mockery of justice and a theatrical display designed to quell dissent and reinforce the authority of the Inquisition, which was controlled by One World Order. Witnesses were coerced into providing false testimony, twisted truths were presented as undeniable facts, and in the end, Father Ignatius was sentenced to death by the most gruesome of means—to be burned at the stake—as a warning to all who dared question their authority.

On the day of his execution, the plaza before the grand cathedral teemed with onlookers, a sea of faces both fearful and curious. The pyre stood tall as its hungry flames licked the skies in anticipation. As Father Ignatius was brought forth, his eyes met those of his accusers without a hint of fear or regret.

As the flames engulfed him, consuming flesh and bone, Father Ignatius spoke not of anger or hatred but of forgiveness. His final words, which were a warning directed to the OWO, echoed through the crackling inferno. "You will not prevail, for I was shown the future, and those who will follow will put an end to your evil plan."

CHAPTER ONE

ASHLEE MARTIN

The sun was beating down on the highway below. Its shine nearly blinded the drivers who were on it. On either side of the highway, sparse vegetation dotted the otherwise barren ground, with its cliff faces jutting out ruggedly and providing an apt background to the plain yet rocky landscape. The summery skies were cloudless and vibrant blue; the breeze was like a hot blaze of air, providing no relief from the stifling seasonal heat. All in all, it was a perfect summer's day.

Ashlee turned the air conditioner of her car to its highest setting and sighed in relief as the sweat glimmering on her brow began to dry. The cool air blew strands of hair, which had begun to mat against her forehead, away from her flushed face and temples.

She had been driving for quite a while. The tug in the pit of her stomach was her only guide to where her destination was. Beyond that, she knew nothing, but she wasn't worried. Her instincts had never led her astray, and she put her complete faith in them. Ashlee still couldn't shake the feeling that her course of action was entirely foolish. *After all*, she thought, *who packs up their entire life in the back of their car and takes off with only a feeling guiding them to where they want to go?* It was preposterous to even think of a move without planning finances, income, residence, and destination.

She had no qualms about it, simply because her instincts were not as shadowy and unclear as the general human population's was. Instead, they were ingrained deeply within her and right down to the marrow of her bones. Over the years, she had honed the feeling to the point that it was second nature to let it guide her in all aspects of her life.

Ashlee Martin had always known that she was different. Since she was a little girl, she could not relate to other children her age. She was not interested in playing games with them. Her parents also noticed that occasionally, she would speak in a language that they couldn't understand but that Ashlee seemed to be very natural and comfortable with. They would ask her what it meant, and she would state that she didn't know what or why she had said it.

On many occasions, she approached people who were physically ill or mentally distraught, and upon touching them, they seemed to improve and become at peace. She was the seventh generation of an only female child, the same as her mother, maternal grandmother, and four prior maternal generations.

As she was growing up in Los Angeles, her interests were conditioning her body and disciplining her mind. She would frequent a fitness center or meditate at the local yoga center when not in classes. She always felt the impulse to help people, which occasionally got her in trouble.

Ashlee grew up to be a beautiful woman with shoulder-length, wavy, dark hair, olive-colored skin, and brown eyes. She had a perfectly shaped body and extremely strong muscles, but she was very feminine and sensual. She always dressed fashionably and appropriately for the occasion but felt more comfortable in formfitting, casual clothes—black being her favorite color.

She was never much into jewelry. She only owned a gold medal which had the archangel Saint Michael on one side and the figure of a bearded person wearing a flounced skirt and a cone-shaped hat with a horned crown on the reverse side. Her mother told her she should always wear it because it would protect and guide her through life. It was very precious to her because it was the only possession she had that had belonged to her mother.

Her mother had told her that their ancestors had come from the Old World and the New World. Her ancestors were from very ancient civilizations, who had mystical knowledge that they used to help humanity. She came from a lineage of very special women with incredible abilities. Her mother told her that her guardian spirit would let her know when the time came for her purpose in life. She never gave these words much importance because she was like most teenagers—only interested in current times and places. Thinking back, she did remember seeing her mother helping people when they were sick. When they sought her help, and she performed strange rituals on them, which seemed mysterious and magical because the person she treated stood up afterward, smiled, and felt well.

When her mother called her to come and eat, she didn't know whether her mother actually called her or if she just imagined it. It was also strange how her mother always somehow knew what she was thinking and anticipated her movements. Now that Ashlee was thinking about it, she didn't recall seeing her mother or father ever being sick, angry, or upset. They were always happy, loving, and very understanding with her.

But even if she wanted to know more, it was too late to ask; her parents had passed away a few years ago in a car accident. After that, she came to realize that they had been a great support for her and how much she loved and missed them. She decided it was time to take her life more seriously, so she enrolled and went on to college, where she obtained a degree in liberal arts with a major in world history and geography.

Other than that, she was an expert in meditation, martial arts, and ancient cultures. She didn't quite know why she needed this knowledge or training, but she sensed that it would come in handy later in life. At this point in life, she had accepted her extra sense and had let it take over all aspects of her life.

After college, she worked various jobs in marketing, which was followed by a job at a movie production studio. She was at the tourist information office for a few years. One day, she met a middle-aged woman traveler, and upon shaking her hand, she felt a jolt of energy. She always had the ability to sense other people's energies and feelings, almost to the point where she could even gather their thoughts and tell what they were thinking and feeling. The woman smiled and said, "Yes, I'm a psychic, and I also can sense your energy. You have an important destiny to fulfil; follow your path." Soon after that, Ashlee concluded that it was time to move on. She could also sense a strong energy from specific locations. It almost felt as if these places were calling and pulling her there. She had been resisting this energy for a long time.

In all honesty, she had not let her peculiar senses fully take the wheel. She had just let them affect her interactions. But now, she was ready to dive in and drive into the great unknown. She expected to feel anxious, but she didn't know why, considering that she had never felt that way when she decided to abide by her instincts. Thankfully, she felt at peace; the mounting anxiety she had experienced over the years was due to her neglecting to follow her instincts. Had she known this, she would have followed it a lot sooner.

This was how she knew it was time to give in, follow the pull of the energy that she felt, and find out once and for all what it was about. This was how she found herself driving to the town of Sedona, Arizona, on this beautiful, clear, sunny day in October. She'd never been there, but the attraction and energy coming from this direction were quite strong. Somehow, she knew it was her destination.

She had exited Interstate 17 and was on State Highway 179 toward Sedona when she felt a strong energy surge, which gave her goose bumps that had nothing to do with the cool air blasting straight at her from the vents. She knew it was the right direction, especially as she entered town.

As she continued to drive, the scenery remained desertlike— similar to how it had been her whole drive to this town with unknown possibilities. She admired the scenery. As the sun began to set, she watched the skies turn a stunning blend of orange, red, and yellow. The road stretched ahead of her, leading her to a new home. She felt a pull to the right when she approached the junction of State Highway 89.

She turned and followed the road for less than two blocks, slowing down to appreciate the quaint little town. She saw people milling about and entering and exiting multiple shops. She seemed to have entered the shopping complex of the town, for which she was glad. She needed to check out this place to find a job and bed to crash in for the night and to grab a bite to eat. She was starving. Having been on the road since the crack of dawn, her breakfast was a distant memory.

She soon reached a roundabout and took a left. Somehow, her eyes fell on the sign of an open café, which had a few patrons visible from its windows. The sign read "Macy's Café," and the place looked old but not rundown. The redbrick establishment evoked a sense of home in her and that she had arrived.

Ashlee parked her car in front of it. Her car was a few years old but was very reliable. It was a dark-gray Ford sedan with a black interior, which was very comfortable and easy to drive. It had an excellent sound system, which was important because she loved to listen to music, and a great air-conditioning system, which made it very comfortable for long rides.

When she opened the car door, she was assaulted by a blast of warm evening air and heady aromas of delicious food, which wafted from the café. They encouraged her to quicken her steps to sate her hunger. She shut the door and locked it because it contained all her possessions and some sentimental family items that she did not want to be stolen.

As her body began to acclimate to the temperature, she realized that the air had cooled with the setting of the sun, which allowed her to dally, take a few deep breaths, and stretch her legs after the long drive. She could have made pit stops, but she didn't want to allow herself to turn back or change her mind. She also couldn't rid herself of the urgency to get where she had to go—which she now knew was this town. She wondered what was calling her here and then dismissed the thought altogether. She wasn't too worried about it; things tended to reveal themselves in their own time, and she could be patient.

As she headed inside, the tinkling of the bell announced her entrance, causing the other patrons to look her way. They eyed her curiously, much in the way that small-town people who knew one another could always spot a newbie amongst them. Ashlee paid it no mind. She smiled at anyone she locked eyes with. Most of them smiled back while some of them looked away. She took a booth close to the entrance, and a waitress came over almost immediately.

The waitress was pushing forty, and she had a pinup-girl air about her. Ashlee felt a tingling sensation, and images rushed to her head, as she got a read on the waitress's energy and thoughts. She could tell that she was a good person, even without her extra senses and just from her crinkling, warm, brown eyes and wide, welcoming smile.

Ashlee had always had the ability to sense other people's energy and feelings, almost to the point where she could even gather their thoughts—a suggestion, to word it better—to tell what they were thinking and feeling. She could even identify the "thinker" as each of them had his or her own distinct voice, which she grew familiar with as she spent more time with that person.

"Hello there. My name's Cindy; you look like you've been on the road for a while. Can I get you something to drink and eat?"

"Yes, please," said Ashlee, returning the smile. "I haven't had a look at the menu, but I would like to order your biggest burger, a healthy helping of fries, a tall strawberry milkshake, and a piece of apple pie, if you have any?"

The waitress chuckled in a friendly manner. "Of course, we do," Cindy replied, "I'll be right back with your order." And with that, she walked away.

Ashlee whiled the short wait away by people watching through the window on her right, only turning when she sensed the waitress was returning to her table with her order. Ashlee gave a cursory glance at the table and felt her mouth water. She gazed up at the waitress and expressed her gratitude, to which Cindy grinned before turning toward another customer, who had just entered the café. A shiver crawled up her spine, and she whipped around to see what had caused it. No one who stood out to her until her attention went to the gentleman whom Cindy was attending to. She was unable to see him, seeing as he was seated in the booth behind her, but she could sense the energy he emitted. It was hard to miss, and she didn't know what to make it.

Ashlee shook her head to dismiss the feeling, choosing to analyze it after putting some food into her system. She dug into her meal and ate it with gusto, demolishing her early supper and late lunch until all that was left was her decadent slice of apple pie, which she enjoyed at a leisurely pace, now that her stomach was comfortably full.

Cindy came over to collect her plate, and Ashlee took this opportunity to learn more about the place and get a head start on her job and apartment hunting. "I just arrived in your beautiful town, and I feel like it's the perfect place to live. Can you recommend any place where I can stay for the night and rent out to live in permanently, or do you know anyone hiring help? I'm a fast learner and can do almost anything, plus I am really good at dealing with people, sales, etc."

Cindy nodded eagerly. "I'll ask around if anyone is looking for help, and I'll let you know. I believe there are a few places that have had recent openings for jobs. Just give me your cell phone number. In the meantime, if you're looking for a place to stay, come and check out where I live: the New Age Home for single women." Ashlee chuckled a little at the name. "It's around the corner, and there's still one room available for rent," Cindy continued. "It's very comfortable and homey, and it has five other single female tenants other than yours truly. It's also safe and includes utilities, and a very kind, smart businesswoman owns it."

This pleased Ashlee greatly. "Perfect! I'll do that. Thank you very much." Her attention went back to the man sitting in the next booth. She had felt a strong energy surge the moment that he walked by her, which was stronger than the one she had felt before. She didn't want to turn to see him, but she could sense his presence and attraction. After clearing the bill, she bit her lip contemplatively, stood up, and turned.

CHAPTER TWO

THE TEACHER

"**A**nd that's it! Good session, guys. I'll see you all next week!" Joe said with a smile before rolling up his yoga mat. Many came over to shake his hand and ask questions about certain poses while others waved before leaving.

"Hey there, handsome. The night's still young. Want to come down with me for a few drinks?" The feminine purring drove his attention away from the man he had just bid farewell to. Yet he knew exactly who it was before he even turned to look.

Mentally sighing, he turned around with a polite smile toward the tall blond who was smiling seductively back at him. Her catty green eyes casually perused his frame with a come-hither look. "I'm flattered, Natasha, but I must decline. I have a few errands to run," Joe answered, maintaining a friendly tone yet being careful not to sound overly inviting.

Natasha Ferguson had joined his classes around two months ago. She had been pestering him to go out with her ever since. Despite giving her clear hints, she refused to acknowledge them and tried again. Joe knew he should tell her a clear, "No," but he could not find it in himself to be rude to the woman. And much to his chagrin, this tiresome cycle continued. Natasha pouted. He was sure she was trying to be cute. However, he couldn't find a single attractive feature about her. *Natasha is good-looking,* he thought, *and confident. But hitting on me is getting old.*

"Come on, Joey. You always make excuses. Just this once, please?" she batted her eyelashes at him as he barely kept himself from grimacing.

He nearly cringed. *God, I hate that nickname.* Fixing an apologetic smile on his face, he declined again. "Sorry, Natasha, I just can't. It's important."

She sighed, and with an eye roll, she backed off. Joe had just begun to sigh in relief when she leaned in close and placed her hand on his chest. "But I will try again. You better say yes." She winked. Joe inwardly groaned. With that, she turned around, and her ponytail swayed left and right as she sashayed out of the room.

"Damn it," he muttered under his breath, rubbing his face before tidying the room. Once that was done, he showered in the bathroom en suite attached to his office before changing into some street clothes. Once he had dressed, he made his way to the door.

He walked past his bookshelf, which contained some of his books on ancient civilizations, and thought about how much they had helped increase his mental awareness and clarity. He was now able to focus on finding answers to specific questions that he had had since childhood, such as were we created, what's our purpose in life, what's our future fate, and does God exist? But it seemed that no matter how much he read and researched, he just couldn't find the answers that he was looking for. He always had the feeling that something was missing and that a veil was over his mind preventing him from being completely aware. He had the sensation that certain places on Earth were pulling him there, and it wasn't clear to him why.

He walked out of the center, locked it behind him, and then began to make his way to Macy's. His stomach grumbled at the promise of food. All that yoga had worked up a mean appetite, and he was ready to eat a horse.

As he walked toward the café, he reflected on how he had decided to settle down in Sedona. His mind wandered back to the time when he had been driving down Route 40 into Arizona, which had been the old Route 66 highway. He had been on the road for weeks heading west, stopping at whatever town he was in by nightfall. He was in his white Mercedes-Benz SUV, which he had owned for a few years, but that was the first time he really enjoyed all of its features. It had a great premium sound system, which he enjoyed because he loved to listen to music. It had plush, comfortable seats and a very good air-conditioning system.

As he was approaching Flagstaff, his initial thought was to spend the night there, but when he saw the sign for Highway 89 to Sedona, he knew immediately that it was where he had to go. He recalled feeling an intense pull and excitement and knew this was his destination. He arrived at night and booked a hotel room, feeling tired but happy to be there.

He remembered that on the following morning while having an early breakfast at Macy's Café, he had an inspirational idea: He would open a yoga and meditation center and teach the wonderful techniques he had learned, all of which had helped him so much throughout his life. He felt this immense energy around him. He also felt that he was meant to be there and to wait, but to wait for what or whom, he didn't know.

When the waitress came over to ask if there was anything else she could get for me, he remembered looking at her and asking, "Yes. Who can I ask about renting an office space around here?"

She smiled, nodded, and replied, "Yes, I know just the person for you to talk to; she's a local real-estate agent and knows all the available places." She wrote down the name and gave it to him, saying, "My name's Cindy. Let me know if there's anything else you need." He thanked her and left to find the agent, and the rest was history. It was hard to imagine that several years had already gone by since then.

Now, as he was looking forward to a good dinner, a thrill went through him as he neared the café. He stopped walking and frowned in confusion. He breathed in deeply and closed his eyes before opening up his senses to his surroundings. Immediately like a honing beacon, he felt a magnetic pull of energy nearly dragging him toward it. He also had an incredible sensation of well-being and an increase of strength and mental awareness. The intensity was heady to the point where it left him nearly tipsy and made him sway in his place.

He opened his eyes and sighed. His eyes were riveted to Macy's Café. It's where the energy signature was coming from. He began walking purposefully again until he was in front of the doors. He felt a flutter of nerves, and his skin turned to gooseflesh from the charge he sensed. He opened the door, heard the bell tinkle, and looked around. Instantly, he spotted the reason for his imbalance and attraction. Joe couldn't see her face, but she had shoulder-length, wavy, black, glossy hair, which shined even in the dull light of the café. Her shoulders were dainty but wide, and they peeked out from under her sleeveless tank top. Her skin was a warm tan color, which looked smooth to the touch. He found himself intrigued and attracted to her, wondering absently if she could sense it too.

"Oh! Hey, Joe, want the usual?" Cindy asked with a smile.

"Yes, please. How have you been?" Joe asked, smiling back.

"Oh, I feel renewed, especially after that wonderful pose you taught me to work out that kink in my back. I'll be right back with your order." With that, she rushed off.

He leaned back in his seat and focused on the woman in front of him. Closing his eyes again, he felt the gentle hum of her aura and energy. Titillated, he brushed it with his own. His eyes snapped open in surprise when the energy flared, and he saw the woman sit up straighter. *Can she sense me?*

Cindy returned with his food, and he dug in. However, his ears perked up when the woman stopped Cindy. Her husky voice was feminine and low. He found himself wanting to hear her speak more. He could hear her conversation with Cindy and her that say she was looking for work. Well then, it seemed that he would be making introductions sooner rather than later. He needed to know this woman, and he needed to work out what was up.

By the time she stood up, he had finished his food and placed a generous tip for Cindy and the money for his order on the table. He did not plan on dallying or letting this woman get away from him. He needed to know who she was. He couldn't explain it, but he felt that he needed to know. He took in a deep, steadying breath as she turned.

CHAPTER THREE

THE ENCOUNTER

His breath whooshed out of him as their gazes locked and time stood still. He had never seen such a stunning pair of eyes before. They were a deep warm brown, enrapturing him so that he could not look away. One might say that he was attracted immensely, and while he would readily agree with that observation, this was not mere attraction or infatuation. Even if it appeared to be simple and surface level, this magnetic pull had much more depth to it. It originated from both their energies seeming to be so drawn toward each another.

Her lips were pulled up into a small smile, soft and demure, and he thought she looked enchanting. She also looked quite young and seemed strong and fit. He could tell that she engaged in physical pursuits, and he admired that in her. He considered himself a tall guy at six feet four inches. He often had to look down at most people. But she came up his nose. A subtle glance at her feet told him she had on a nice pair of suede boots with high heels. Still, he could tell she was a tall woman, which was yet another trait he found quite attractive.

He saw that she was on the brink of passing him by, so he quickly said, "Hello, my name is Joe. I couldn't help hearing that you are looking for a job. I own a yoga meditation center here in town called the Yoga Energy Center, and I'm looking for someone to help me run it. Are you interested?" Joe had not planned to offer her a job—at least not immediately. But he didn't regret it. He could feel a charge around him from his energy interacting with hers. Not for the first time that evening, he wondered if she could sense it too.

When he looked into her eyes, he couldn't help but feel another bout of attraction toward her. She was a gorgeous, young woman, and a part of him was slightly miffed as she appeared much younger than him. For the life of him, though, he couldn't say why. He also had this intense sense that they should be together, and he couldn't deny it. In what capacity remained to be seen. He just hoped she would say yes. He had no other means to ensure a second meeting; although he was not against thinking up other avenues of subtle persuasion.

★★★

Ashlee looked up at Joe, observing he was tall and handsome. He was possibly a man who was very popular with his peers and the ladies. He dressed casually but with good taste. Again, she sensed an intense energy surge and a pull toward him, which she was finding harder and harder to resist. It was becoming quite challenging to resist him and the lure of his energy, which seemed to seep into and mingle with hers, creating this static buzz in the air.

It didn't help that he was a fine male specimen. Albeit lean, he was packing sinewy muscles, which showed through his casual T-shirt and jeans. He had unruly black curls, deep brown eyes, and a dimpled smile that caused her heart to beat erratically. His cherubic appearance gave him a youthful air, but he was a manly man, whom she found pleasant.

She was quite grateful for the abrupt yet irresistible offer, even if she found it strange that he had been eavesdropping. Although she couldn't fault him seeing as he had been seated right behind her. Smiling, she said, "Nice to meet you, Joe. I'm Ashlee. Thank you so much. It's very kind of you to offer me a job. I accept," and shook his hand. Upon touching him, she felt an augmented energy flow with an electrical charge, which zapped her from the point of contact down to her very nerve endings. Immediately, they let go of each other's hands with a startled exclamation and a smile before chuckling.

"That was weird," Joe said.

"Yes," Ashlee said, nodding. Ashlee backed up a step, slightly jittery from the intense spark. It sure gave new meaning to the phrase sparks fly. "I'll get going. I still need to arrange housing, and it's getting late," Ashlee said.

"By all means." Joe indicated the door with an outstretched arm and a charming smile that was dimpled adorably. He took a step back.

The two walked out the door and bid each other goodnight. They had agreed to meet in the meditation center on the following day.

Ashlee then drove over to New Age Home, which had been suggested by Cindy. She was pleasantly surprised to find that not only was it close by but also that she got a room on the second floor. It was of adequate size, and it had a comfortable bed, sitting area, and closet. She had her own bathroom, a small microwave, and a refrigerator, which she loved very much. So within the space of an hour, she had a home with a bunch of other wonderful ladies. She was also happy knowing that she was in the right place and was looking forward to her new life there.

The next morning was bright and sunny, and Ashlee enjoyed it as she made her way to the yoga center. When she opened the door and went in, she observed several women and men working through their yoga routines.

Joe spotted her immediately and greeted her. "Hi! Welcome to my center."

"Nice to be here," she answered with a smile, looking around. "Nice place you've got here," she said before locking eyes with him.

"Thanks," he replied. But Ashlee wasn't paying attention to the conversation. She was trapped in his gaze as their energies mingled and created a heady buzz around her. It was hard for her to pay attention to anything else when they were this close to each other, but she managed to shake it off.

"Come. I'll show you the ropes and give you a formal tour." Joe explained what her duties were, and soon, they both went to work.

★★★

Later in the day after Joe had finished teaching his yoga classes and all the clients had left, he approached Ashlee, who was at the reception desk, and greeted her. "Hi! How did it go on your first day?"

She grinned at him and answered, "Great! I love dealing with your clients. I get nothing but good vibes from almost all of them."

Joe returned her grin. "Good, I'm happy you feel comfortable here, but you said almost all of them. Were there any people you didn't get good vibes from?"

"Well, yes," she replied thoughtfully, pursing her lips to the side, and Joe found his eyes straying to the tiny movement before he pulled his eyes back up to hers. "There's one woman that I feel has intense negative vibes—the tall, blond lady."

Even before she described the woman, Joe knew who she was talking about. "Did she give you a hard time?" he asked seriously, knowing he would have some choice words with Natasha if she dared to toe this line. It was one thing to harass him. It was another to harass his employees.

She chuckled and shook her head. "Nothing I couldn't handle. She just glowered at me from time to time and gave me the attitude—petty playground bully tactics." She rolled her eyes playfully, making him laugh.

The more she spoke, the more he found himself liking her. "Have you ever practiced meditation, yoga, or martial arts?" asked Joe.

"Oh, yes," she answered enthusiastically and then told Joe her life story.

Joe was fascinated to learn all about her. His interest in her deepened as she spoke. He wanted to tell her how he felt, now that he knew she, too, could sense energies. She wouldn't take it the wrong way. "I have a confession to make. I felt this attraction to you the moment I met you, and I couldn't ignore it. Don't get me wrong; you're beautiful, but it's more than that. I can sense your intense energy, which makes me feel stronger. I believe our energy fields are synchronized and feed each other."

"I think so too. I felt the same way."

Ashlee's casual reply helped him heave a mental sigh of relief.

She understands. Joe gave her a mischievous look. "Why don't we experiment a little? Let's practice some martial arts' moves together and see what happens. What do you say?"

"I'm game." She grinned.

★★★

They went to the room that was now vacant of his students and warmed up before they practiced moving against each other. They began slowly at first but gradually became faster. Their hands, arms, and feet slashed at each other in defense and offense. They could easily anticipate each other's moves, as if they could read each other's minds and know what moves to initiate or counteract. This continued for several minutes, and it soon became clear that neither of them could outdo the other, no matter what they tried.

Finally, Joe said, "Enough," and they both stopped, panting slightly. He then grinned with a look of pure amazement on his face. "This is incredible. It's as if your movements and mine are a continuation of each other, and I know what's to follow."

Ashlee said, "Yes, I had the same experience. What does this mean? What's happening to us?"

Joe, who had been practicing meditation and studying religious, metaphysical, and mystic teachings for many years, explained, "I believe we are soul partners; that is, our energies are vibrating at the same frequency. Therefore, whenever we're near each other, it travels between us, back and forth. That's why we get the energy surges and that feeling of well-being. If I'm right, we should be able to link our energy fields and create one strong energy point. Do you want to try it?"

"Yes," said Ashlee excitedly. "What do we do?"

"First, let's dim the lights. Then we will sit back-to-back on one of the yoga mats." After they had assumed this position, Ashlee found his warmth and latent strength against her back to be comforting. He instilled peace and safety in her core. Immediately, she felt her muscles relax and her mind calm down. "Now, I want you to hold my right hand with your left hand and my left hand with your right hand, OK?"

"OK," said Ashlee. This time, there was no spark. However, she felt a gentle hum and a tingle on her skin from the point of contact.

Joe then explained to Ashlee that the energy from their bodies traveled out through their right hands and entered their bodies through their left hands. "I need you to enter a complete relaxation meditation and build up the energy within your body by absorbing the Shakti or prana. This is the cosmic life energy that surrounds us animates all forms of life, maintains the balance of the entire cosmos, and is the source of kundalini, the energy that travels up through our bodies. We will then channel it out our right hands and back in through our left hands. Continue this until you hear me say, 'Go!' Then quickly channel and send it to a point just above our heads. Are you ready?"

She nodded. "Ready."

They entered a state of meditation, absorbing surrounding energy and sending it to each other in a closed circuit. This continued for a few minutes, and then Joe yelled, "Go!" They quickly sent it up through their bodies to a point above their heads. Suddenly, a ball of energy started forming, which had an intense glow, static sparks, and noises. This energy continued growing until it suddenly dissipated after a huge flash.

Ashlee started laughing and in amazement exclaimed, "Wow! That was intense. For a second, I felt the power—like I was connected to the whole world and enlightened with knowledge beyond my own. It felt great!"

Joe laughed and said, "I knew it the moment we met. We're balance partners and soulmates. We were meant to find each other for a reason. I sense that we must accompany and help guide each other to fulfill our destiny; you are a light worker as I am."

She felt her heart flutter at his words despite knowing that they were meant to be platonic. She asked, "What do you mean by balance partners, soulmates, and fulfill my destiny, and what's a light worker?"

Joe smiled and said, "Well, I have to start from the beginning. Let's see; where should I begin?" Joe turned to face her before he proceeded to answer Ashlee's questions. "When balance partners meet, it seems to be by accident, but it's not because the souls guide the meeting. The recognition is immediate by both partners, and the connection forms instantly. We attract each other because we are on the same frequency and have things to share. The synchronicities that develop between balance partners stagger the mind. Balance Partners can be of the same or opposite sex, as this is not about romance but spirituality. Balance partners are in each other's lives to carry out what our souls are here to do now. Spiritually, we enhance each other's growth and can trigger each other's awareness. You have half of the information needed, and I, as your balance partner, have the other half."

"Oh, wow! exclaimed Ashlee. "Is this the reason we seem to complement each other and increase our energies?"

Joe replied, "Yes, absolutely. And a soulmate is when two souls have shared significant past lives together. As they meet again in this life, they are inexplicably drawn to each other and are bonded extraordinarily. Soul partners are specifically designed to help support each other emotionally, professionally, or in any other way required to accomplish whatever our souls need to do here on Earth. Light workers, also called crystal babies, indigos, Earth angels, or star seeds, are spiritual beings who feel an enormous urge to help others. Throughout their lives, they feel great kindness and compassion toward others. Chances are that they've helped people or other living beings in distress from a young age. They volunteer as a beacon for the Earth and commit to serving humanity."

Ashlee interrupted Joe and said, "Now I know why one time in junior high school, I stopped a school bully, who was much bigger than me, from picking on another student. I broke his nose."

Joe smiled and said, "Well, I guess that fits, but in general, light workers are sensitive; they feel sadness and anguish for the misery in their world. This is why they tend to choose professions where their empathetic natures can assist those in need like nursing, medicine, therapy, rehabilitation, healing, caregiving, veterinary services, research, and teaching, etc. They are intuitive and driven by their internal guidance. They can perceive the emotions and needs of other living beings, which enables them to harness and direct their healing powers toward those who need help. They also can expel negative energy and consciousness using their positive energies and healing powers.

"As for your destiny, I don't know what it is, but it must have been imperative that we be brought together. Usually, a light worker's purpose on Earth is to elevate humankind's collective consciousness and well-being, or as in our case, maybe it's something of more vital importance, I don't know. You may not know the reason for your calling right away; it may take some guidance, self-realization, and discovery to find your mission on Earth at this time."

Despite his explanation to her, he admitted to himself that he felt a connection to her. Things were not as black and white as he had stated, but he was in no rush to get into anything. He knew that if it was meant to be, the energies in the cosmos would organically let this happen, and he was patient.

Ashlee nodded, looking pensive. "I understand now why I had all those past experiences. I feel that it has brought you and me to this place. I don't know the reason yet, but I sense we'll find out soon. In the meantime, we should practice combining our energies because it can make us stronger and help us increase our abilities and awareness."

Joe gave her a crooked smile. "Yes, I agree with you. We'll also practice martial arts, meditation, projecting our thoughts to others, and whatever else we discover we can do. We'll continue working during the day as usual so that we don't raise any suspicions; we don't know what or who we're up against, but after hours, we'll continue our teachings."

They said goodnight to each other and went their separate ways. Ashlee pondered everything they had learned and experienced and wondered where this was leading to.

In the following days, Ashlee continued her routine, working during the day and practicing at night with Joe. It had only been a few days, and already, she noticed an increased ability to read people's thoughts, project mental commands to others, and especially, synchronize and combine their energies to create a large energy ball of light during their meditation, which gave them increased awareness.

One night, they also discovered that while in meditation and with the ball of light above their heads, they could will their inner spirits or souls up and through the ball of light to hover high above their bodies in a plane composed of energy and thousands of light points. They found that they could combine them into one, with both of their consciousness within it acting as one while simultaneously keeping their individual awareness. This was a terrifying experience and at the same time, very exhilarating. They had the impression that the light they created was a being with a consciousness and identity of its own, but it was too weak to make itself known. They also discovered that they could tap into this cosmic energy for knowledge and travel within the astral plane, but they decided to take it slowly until they could be sure it was safe and something they could control.

CHAPTER FOUR

THOMAS

It was March of 1985, and a new open-minded individual was appointed general secretary of the Communist party of the Soviet Union. This provided our President with a reliable negotiating partner. A series of summits and high-profile encounters followed. At Reykjavik in October of 1986, they discussed the prospect of abolishing all nuclear weapons. In December of 1987, they signed the Intermediate-Range Nuclear Forces Treaty, which eliminated an entire class of missiles. In May of 1988, while standing in the middle of Red Square in Moscow, our president declared that the term *evil empire* belonged to another era. The world was changing, and because of this, US troops were being reassigned to sensitive areas.

Thomas Patterson was in his office, looking over possible squadrons and their profiles to forward to his superiors. He leaned back in his seat with a tired sigh, and before long, he found himself pondering his life—not for the first time. He was feeling restless and unfulfilled, yet by all standards, he was a success. Thomas was a thirty-four-year-old major in the army. He was a fine-looking man, who always dressed in a military uniform or a two-piece suit. He had an average middle-class upbringing in a loving family and had three married siblings. He never married because he joined the army at eighteen and went to college on a government loan, where he obtained a degree in business administration.

He joined the army because he wanted to make it a career, which was coming up to sixteen years. He was in army intelligence and was very good at it. He was planning to remain there for the rest of his life. He worked round the clock and refrained from socializing. He had no time to meet women. In his position as major of being in charge of the counter-terrorism division had made him very familiar with the intelligence community, not only in his native country but also globally. He had personally participated in numerous missions, especially in his career's initial years.

Now, he was mostly at his desk in his office, directing his department, overseeing younger officers, and carrying out precisely the missions he had planned and received approval for. At this point in life, he debated whether to remain single or to try to find a companion with whom he could share the day's events, trust with all his vulnerabilities and secrets without fear of judgment or divulgence, and talk and laugh with; someone who would care about him. While he loved what he did, there was a hollowness him; part of his life was bleak.

I wonder if I should remain single, he thought. I feel so alone. *Everyone is with someone and seems so settled. I hate the empty house. If only there was someone.*

Suddenly, his office phone rang, and he picked it up. "Hello, Major Patterson speaking."

A clear, deep male voice responded from the other end. "Major Patterson, how would you like to help me save the world?"

He took the receiver away from his ear and gave it a puzzled stare. This was a private military number, so this couldn't possibly be a prank call. Placing it back to his ear, he sternly asked, "Who is this, and how did you get this number?"

"That's not important, but my good friend the president thinks highly of you and believes you're the man for the job. So again, I repeat, how would you like to help me save the world?"

Thomas paused and pondered before answering. "If the president knows this job and sent you to me, it must be for a good cause, so I'm listening."

"Good, I will send you the information about where to meet with

ANUNNAKI

me. I'll explain everything to you then, and after that, you can decide if you'd like to take the job. See you then." With that said, he hung up.

Later that day, Thomas found himself in a local hotel room. He had received an envelope with the hotel name, room number, and room key. He was instructed to be there at 8:00 p.m. and to turn on the TV monitor. As soon as he did, the display showed a shadow, and the voice he had heard earlier began speaking. "Welcome. For our security, you will only hear my voice and not know my identity. And through a secret number that only you will have, you can call me any time."

Thomas raised a brow but remained silent. Then he asked, "Well, that's great. But what is this about? I don't even know why I would want to call you."

"I'm a very, very wealthy person, and I also represent a conglomerate of five super-wealthy persons, who control multinational corporations. We have unlimited resources and finances that I want to put at your disposal."

"All right, I'll bite. Why would you want to do that?"

I'll tell you why. Some time ago, I was approached by an evil organization called the One World Order. They wanted to recruit me for their organization. They are an ancient secret society, which was formed in biblical times. Angry and scared of losing her kingdom after the great world flood, the widow of Nimrod, the king of Babel, offered her unborn baby to Satan so that he could walk on this earth again.

With his help, she ruled and started the worship of Baal, the representative of Satan, who upon her death, took control of the secret society, which he has maintained since then. Their main goal was and is to reestablish a one-world government or kingdom, which he would lead and be in full control of. He plans to challenge God when he returns because he was left behind and stripped of his position. Before the war in heaven, he was the right hand of God and commander of his legion of angels. But after the expulsion, he was condemned to remain in the astral plane until the end of time, awaiting his judgment and fate. He would not accept that and conspired to regain his freedom and prepare for the coming confrontation. I need someone in charge of the group I have put together to fight this evil."

Thomas's eyes went wide before he became angry. *What does this guy take me for?* "Wow! That sounds like a fairy tale or science fiction story. Am I supposed to believe all this about the devil, the conspiracy to control the world, and a secret society?" Thomas started to get up, and only the mystery man's next words gave him a pause.

"I have proof."

Thomas stopped and turned to the monitor, asking, "What proof?"

"We have ancient relics that used to belong to Father Crespi, who was assigned to a parish in Cuenca, Ecuador. Are you familiar with the area?"

"Yes, I am. You know I'm in the army intelligence division."

"His relics prove that the gods visited us and that they once walked among us. The One World Order wanted them, but we got them before they did. They hold the secret of how to fight this evil organization, so we need to use them. I want to fly you out to our secret facility and have you examine them. If afterward, you think it is science fiction, you'll get paid $250,000 for your troubles, and you will be flown back to your base. Is this acceptable to you?"

Thomas was flabbergasted. He asked, "You're serious, aren't you?"

"Yes, I am."

"OK," said Thomas, "I'll go with you, and after I see these so-called relics, I'll give you my answer."

"Good," replied the voice. "An SUV is waiting for you downstairs to take you to the airport and our facility—"

"Wait a minute. I have to ask permission from my superior officer before I can go anywhere."

"Oh, do not worry! That has already been taken care of," the voice said, assuring him instantly. "As of now, you have a three-day pass authorized by your superior officer, which I hope to make permanent by you joining us."

With a surprised expression, Thomas asked, "How did you manage that?"

"Didn't I mention that the president is a good friend of mine?" the man said after giving a half-suppressed laugh.

"Of course, right, let's go," Thomas replied with a laugh.

An ebony-colored SUV was downstairs and waiting outside the main entrance. Thomas got in to drive off to the airport, where a private jet would be awaiting him. On the way he thought, *If the president and this mysterious person has faith in my ability to carry out this mission, it will be my duty to all humankind to at least try.*

Soon after reaching the airport, he boarded the jet and put his seat belt on before it took off. Once in the air, a flight attendant, after greeting him, said, "Welcome, Major Patterson. Would you like something to drink or eat before you get some sleep? It will be a six-hour-long flight?"

"Yes, miss. Thank you."

Once he had finished eating, the flight attendant provided him with a blanket and a pillow. Soon, Thomas was asleep.

Awhile later, the flight attendant delicately announced, "We have arrived at JFK airport in New York." He was still groggy but surprised to learn where he had arrived at. He exited the plane, and another black SUV awaited him there.

He was taken to New York City and downtown Manhattan. They dropped him off at the front entrance to a mammoth skyscraper. There, he was met by a young man in a black suit, who said, "Please follow me, Major." He was led into a high-tech elevator with a secret button to the basement, which was several stories underground. In a few seconds, the elevator door ripped apart, making an opening for Thomas to walk out.

"This is incredible," he blurted out.

Then he saw a sleek and smiling woman, who extended her hand to Thomas in greeting. "Hi! Welcome to our center. I'm Mary. We are delighted to meet you. We were told to take you directly to the laboratory where we have the ancient relics from Father Crespi, so please follow me. By the way, I'm in charge of our facility's computer systems and communications. I was instructed to take you to our secured conference room afterward, where you will receive a call from our patron. Do you have any questions?"

"None, thank you." Thomas then proceeded to follow Mary, observing the enormous size of this ultramodern and innovative secret facility, which was underneath an unsuspecting structure in the heart of the city. He was wondering how it came to be.

Mary continued speaking. "You're probably wondering what this place is. Well, this is our headquarters, and it's a secret location that was going to be used as a nuclear fallout shelter and bunker for chief military, government, and civilian personnel, but it never was. It has its own main energy grid or a power source, state-of-the-art computers, satellites, radios, and tele-video communication equipment. It is bombproof, shielded, undetectable by all known means, completely self-contained, and able to house and feed a thousand persons for fifty years. What do you think of our headquarters, Major Patterson?"

"This is an amazing and incredible facility."

"We also have hundreds of vetted, committed, and loyal people, who are specialists in their fields, to carry out our mission. Our location in the heart of a busy New York City permits us to enter and leave without arousing suspicions."

"Hmm." He observed her every word.

"Here we are, Major. This is the lab, and I'm to let you review and examine the relics from Father Crespi at your leisure. I will be accompanying you for security reasons or in case you have any questions."

Thomas nodded, said, "Thank you," and approached a lengthy table with many artifacts on it. There were metal sheets with engravings, statues, pieces of pottery, and many other items. Thomas, due to his background in intelligence, had developed a keen sense when it came to analyzing objects and data and determining if they were authentic or not. He applied himself to his work. He was so focused that nothing in the world could take away his attention. After a few hours, Thomas finally relaxed from his task, and he turned to Mary and asked, "Has anyone else examined these artifacts or been able to decipher the writings."

"Yes. Our experts have dated them to over twelve thousand years. They agreed with Father Crespi; he claimed that they were antediluvian. As for the writing, they're still working on it," Mary said.

Thomas nodded contemplatively before giving her a short smile.

"OK, I'm done for now. Can you please take me to the conference room?"

"Yes. Follow me, please."

Once there, a large screen was turned on, and the familiar figure was on display. "Nice to see you again, Thomas. Did you find the proof you were looking for?"

"OK, you have my attention. I believe the relics to be genuine, and if so, history may need to be rewritten. Also, what's the OWO's interest in these relics, and what do you want me to do?"

"For thousands of years, the One World Order has been trying to take over the world for their evil purpose, even if it means destroying it in the process. Over the years, they have infiltrated every country, government, and organization throughout the world, placing their agents in high places or influential positions. They await the moment to strike a blow and take control of the world. They will not let anything or anyone stand in their way—particularly me. Since I rejected their offer to join them in their evil mission, I have been using all my resources to stop them. So now our organization's agents and I are on their hit list to be terminated on sight. Our headquarters is only known to the people currently working there. We have eight-person teams, which we call cells, throughout the world. They only know one other and no one else in our group. They all communicate and receive orders from this center through their team leaders. For security reasons, we use first names or pseudo names. You have a choice."

"Thomas, I would like for you to be the director and person in charge of the entire group that we call Saving Earth Group or just the Group. Your office will be here at headquarters, and you will be the one to determine what we need to do to stop the OWO. You will be accountable only to me, and all my communications with the group will be through you. Never worry about money; you will have all the necessary resources to accomplish your mission. As for your mission, your primary goal is to save the earth by stopping and eliminating the One World Order secret society. The ancient relics could provide you with the necessary information to accomplish this. That's the reason that OWO wants to get their hands on them—to destroy anything that could lead to their termination. You will be living most of the time in the facility's luxury apartments, and odds are that you will never have a chance to have your own family. But the group would be your family from here on in, so what did you decide?"

Thomas was silent as he thought hard and tried to decide if he wanted to give up his dream of having his own family and a military career for this new challenge, which would pretty much take up all his time. Hence, it left no room for anything else, including marriage. He realized that if the OWO was successful, there would be no world as we know it, so someone must stop them. Maybe this group could be that someone.

He finally smiled and said, "I guess I have a big family now; I'll take it."

The voice shouted, "Great! Major, I knew you would say yes. Mary will convey to everyone that you are in charge now. Also, she'll give you a tour of the entire facility and guide you to your sophisticated apartment. From here on in, you will have control of our entire organization and its resources. Call me any time before sunrise, after sunset, or during the sun's shine because I would like you to keep me informed. One last thing: you will have an honorable discharge from the army effective today. Your superior officer will be informed as the Department of Defense."

"Yes. For the group, I'll give it my all."

THE MEETING

A shlee stood up from behind the desk and stretched to relieve her stiff muscles before straightening. They had just dismissed the afternoon batch of people, and she could finally allow herself a breather. Seeing Joe coming toward her, she smiled.

"Hey, would you like to eat at Macy's for lunch?"

"Sure, I'm starving," she replied before glancing at him. "But let's order using our thought projection, OK?"

Joe's eyes widened before a smile slowly took over his lips. "Sounds good to me," said Joe, and they both laughed.

Ashlee and Joe had been training together for almost a month. They had harnessed skills so that their thought projection could target anyone and any location. Their mind reading had improved drastically while their out-of-body astral projection was getting easier.

Ashlee kept feeling an alien sensation though. She felt the presence of someone else when they merged their energies in the astral plane, but it was not defined. There was no ill intent, so she wasn't too concerned. She discussed it with Joe, and she was surprised to learn that he had been experiencing the same thing.

Ashlee had also begun to take comfort in Joe's company. She was spending quite a lot of time with him at the center for work or practice, at Macy's for mealtime, or simply for other outings beyond these perimeters.

They quickly locked up the center and walked over to the café.

They talked as they went because the two of them had become good friends in the past month. But Ashlee was a little disturbed at feeling so attracted to Joe because she didn't want it to interfere with their work relationship.

They went into the café and sat at a booth while still talking. It wasn't long before Cindy came over, smiling and saying, "Hi, Ashlee. Hi, Joe. What shall I get you guys?" Ashlee exchanged a mischievous look with Joe before she focused her thoughts on Cindy. She felt Joe do the same thing while Cindy was writing. Cindy looked up and said, "OK. I have one BLT and chips and one turkey club sandwich with chips. Is that right?"

"Yes," they answered in unison and smiled.

Cindy then frowned in confusion before shaking her head as though disoriented and said, "It was weird when you placed your orders. I could hear you clearly, but it didn't seem like you were talking very loudly."

They both laughed, and Joe said, "That is weird."

Cindy quickly turned around with the same confused look and went to the kitchen while speaking over her shoulder. "It won't take long."

"Thanks, Cindy," Ashlee replied before exchanging another look and chuckling.

"Think you want to go on another hike tonight?" Joe asked conversationally, and Ashlee's eyes lit up.

"Oh, I'd love to!" she rapidly responded.

Ashlee and Joe enjoyed hiking because several energy centers or subtle energy vortexes were in the Sedona area. The energy from these vortexes saturated the whole area in and around Sedona, and it could be noticed subtly but generally anywhere around town. Going to one of the vortex sites where the energy was most potent could be a very uplifting experience. As Ashlee discovered, the energy you absorb from one of these energy centers could stay with you and affect you positively for days afterward. Four major Sedona vortex sites existed: Cathedral Rock, Bell Rock, Boynton Canyon, and Airport Mesa.

Ashlee and Joe preferred the Bell Rock vortex because it was electromagnetic and had immense quartz crystals within or beneath it, which created a very high energy concentration. The energy was intense. It strengthened all three parts of the spiritual being: masculine, feminine, and balance. The male side revealed a deep regard for the value of your own life while the feminine side revealed a deep concern for the life of others. The maturity of the masculine side was parallel to the feminine side, and it defined the balance between the two. This balance described how they treated others compared to themselves and governed what types of emotions they felt most strongly.

The vortex energy at Bell Rock could enhance their spirits, help them increase new perspectives, and cause them to be more aware of themselves and others, balancing mind, body, and soul. But they had another favorite vortex: the Boynton Canyon-Kachina Vortex, which was an electromagnetic vortex of balanced energies. It was the most mysterious and sacred of the main vortexes in Sedona, Arizona. The energy at this vortex also strengthened all three parts of their spiritual being and masculine and feminine balance, which benefited relationships by maintaining intimacy, honesty, and openness.

In ancient times, the natives would not enter the canyon without first purifying themselves through fasting or deep meditation. The energy there was very balanced and calm. This vortex was grounding and uplifting. It would generate nourishment and strength to recharge and align the mind, body, and spirit.

After a hike to a vortex, they would find themselves literally fully charged. This made their astral projections more intense.

While waiting for Cindy to bring their lunch, Ashlee thought, *It's been six months since I arrived in Sedona. I love how my life is at this moment, and I love spending time with Joe. But I wonder where all this is leading me to.*

Early that morning, they had gone hiking as usual before starting work. But something very curios happened to them as they were ready to head back. Ashlee bent over to get into the car when Joe suddenly exclaimed, "Wait! What's that hanging from your neck?"

Touching the gold chain hanging from her neck, she replied, "I'm not much for jewelry; this is the only piece I own. It's a gold medal of the archangel Saint Michael on one side and the figure of a bearded person wearing a flounced skirt and a cone-shaped hat with a horned crown on the reverse side. According to what my mother explained to me when I was a child, the person is depicted with two streams of water flowing into each of his shoulders. One is the Tigris, and the other is the Euphrates. Alongside him are two trees symbolizing the male and female aspects of nature. An eagle is descending from above to land upon his outstretched right arm. This portrayal reflects his role of overseeing water, life, and replenishment. I never really understood all of this at that time, and I wasn't curious enough to ask more about it. But my mother told me I should always wear it because it would protect me and guide me through life. It's very precious to me since it's the only possession I have of hers."

Joe exclaimed, "Wow! You're not going to believe this," and from under his T-shirt, Joe pulled out an exact replica of the medal.

Now it was Ashlee's turn to exclaim, "Wow! Where did you get that from?"

Joe replied, "I was adopted and raised by a wealthy and highly educated family in Chicago. My adopted parents were very loving and caring. I grew up loving them. I was told at a young age that my mother had died in an accident and that my father was unable to raise me himself. I was told that for my benefit and safety, my father gave me up for adoption. My only link to my parents was this gold medal of the archangel Saint Michael on one side and the figure of a bearded person shown wearing a flounced skirt and a cone-shaped hat with a horned crown on the reverse side of the medal. According to my adoptive parents, my mother had given it to me when I was born and wanted me to wear it always to protect and guide me. As I got older, I always wondered about my birth parents. I decided that one day, I would search for my father and get answers."

Ashlee and Joe stared at each other and then said in unison, "This can't be just a coincidence." Ashlee could sense it was something more profound and linked to them meeting in Sedona. Ashlee could sense Joe feeling the same and pondering what it all meant. They were quiet as they headed back to work.

Later in the day Ashlee had forgotten all about it because she had been feeling perfect all day. She was eager and looking forward to trying an astral projection again later that evening after work.

Once they were done with their lunch hour, they returned to work. It seemed like a long afternoon, but finally, the day ended. It was five, and they were bidding goodbye to the last client of the day. They were busy discussing their hiking plans and were about to close when the door opened. A middle-aged gentleman in a two-piece suit walked in. He was tall and broad-shouldered like a linebacker. His hair was graying at the temples. The corners of his eyes and mouth were slightly wrinkled, but the man was in great shape for his age. That much was clear.

"Hello, my name is Thomas, and I would like a few minutes of your time if I may."

Ashlee looked at Joe, wondering what this was about. Joe stepped forward and shook the proffered hand before he answered, "I'm sorry, but we're closed for the day. If you like, we can see you tomorrow."

Thomas smiled and said, "I'm not here for yoga classes but for both of you, Joe and Ashlee."

Ashlee quickly asked, "Wait, wait. How do you know our names? Do we know you?"

Smiling, Thomas answered, "No, but I know you very well, and I'm hoping we can become good friends. You see, some coworkers of mine and I have been monitoring and observing you for some time. We have discovered and determined that you have incredible energy and abilities, and we would like you to join our group."

As Joe folded his arms, his eyes grew hard, even as he kept his tone polite. "I don't know what you're talking about. And none of us is interested in joining anyone, so thank you, and please leave."

Thomas raised both of his palms in a gesture of surrender. "I understand that you are not trusting me and being cautious. But we know exactly what you are and your capabilities. We know that both of you are good people and that you care about others. We know your abilities. You're probably wondering why you were brought together and where to go from here. Well, I can answer all your questions, but you must come to our group's headquarters and see for yourselves.

I can tell you now that you're both very important for humankind's survival and that you are in danger if you stay here by yourselves."

Joe and Ashlee looked at each other, and they nodded their heads. They had already scanned Thomas's thoughts and knew he was trustworthy and telling the truth. Ashlee was the one to speak to Thomas this time. "OK, we know there's something we have to do, and it seems that our path has taken us to you, so yes, we'll join you."

Thomas raised a brow at Joe, who gave him a nod. Thomas grinned. "Great! I'll have a vehicle pick you up tomorrow. You will not be coming back. I'll have someone come afterward to pack your belongings and close this center for you. You'll see that we have everything you need at our headquarters and more. You will be comfortable and safe with us, so I'll see you tomorrow at our center."

As Thomas turned to leave, Joe halted him with a question. "What's your group's name, and where's the headquarters?"

Thomas gave them a kind smile. "It's best you don't know—for now. But tomorrow, all your questions will be answered. Goodnight, and see you tomorrow." With that, Thomas left just as abruptly as he had come in.

"I wonder what this means for us." Ashlee said.

"Well, we'll figure it out soon enough," Joe responded before looking at Ashlee. The two stared at each other, knowing their lives would change forever.

CHAPTER SIX

THE GROUP

Before waiting outside the yoga center, Ashlee and Joe packed their belongings and ate breakfast at Macy's. Ashlee had let the ladies know that she would be gone indefinitely and to feel free to rent out the space to someone else. They had all been very kind, friendly, and accommodating. They had thrown her a mini going-away party before they had gone to bed. Ashlee was thankful for getting to know such lovely ladies and was sad to go, but she knew it was necessary. Thankfully, the girls had not asked her why she was leaving on such short notice; she hadn't wanted to lie to them.

Joe, too, had tied up loose ends at short notice. He called his manager and left him in charge of the dojo while they remained away. They also had enough instructors to cover Joe's classes while he stayed away. "How do you feel about this?" Joe asked, leaning back against the railing of the steps leading up to the center.

"Honestly, somewhat excited but mostly anxious and a bit nervous. Whatever Thomas told us last night sounded quite serious. And the part where he said our lives are in danger," she said and then pinched her brows and pursed her lips, expressing her distress, before reluctantly saying, "It's making me really concerned about our safety. It's also making me wonder why anyone would be after our lives. We've never hurt anyone, and we have no enemies; at least, none that we know of." Ashlee bit her lip, folded her arms across her chest, and leaned on the opposite railing across from Joe.

"Oh, I don't know. I may have stolen a bag of chips from one of the class bullies back in second grade, a time or two. He might be out to get revenge." Joe shrugged before chuckling.

"That was so lame!" Ashlee laughed.

Joe shrugged again, continuing to chuckle. "It eased the tension, didn't it?" He raised a brow. At her nod, he smiled and spoke again. "I feel the same way you do, to be honest. But I feel like we will be safer with these guys. Something in me tells me they can be trusted."

Ashlee agreed before they saw a black SUV pull up to the curb. "Our ride's here," she announced.

They picked up their luggage and got inside the vehicle. They were taken to the local airport, where they boarded a private jet. This was Ashlee's first time flying in a private jet, and she was very impressed. She let out a spontaneous, "Wow!" when she saw it had several reclining seats, which looked very plush and comfortable. It was spacious, and it had computer monitors and an internet connection for their use. It had two restrooms in the rear, which both had shower facilities.

Joe looked at her, smiled, and said," I'm glad you're enjoying it, but I think we have a long trip ahead of us, so we should try to get some rest."

Ashlee chuckled and replied, "I'll try." But then she found out that it also had excellent food, which was served by two flight attendants, who were very nice and friendly. After eating, she fell into a deep sleep.

The aircraft had a pilot and copilot who kept them informed of their flight status as needed. Ashlee opened her eyes when the pilot announced that they would be arriving in New York City in a few minutes. She looked at Joe, who smiled and gave her a nod.

After they landed, they were transported in another black SUV to a building in downtown Manhattan. Then they were led into an elevator with a secret button to a basement, which was many stories underground.

The elevator door opened, and the two walked out, observing their surroundings in complete awe. "This is unbelievable, amazing!" Joe exclaimed. Joe's eyes fell on Thomas, who stood waiting to greet them.

He nudged Ashlee, who turned and met Thomas's eyes. The two made their way over to him quickly.

Thomas, smiling, extended his hand to Ashlee and Joe and said, "Welcome to our center. I'm delighted you accepted my invitation. I hope to answer all your questions, especially why you're important for our mission and humanity's survival. I'm in charge of this central facility as the mission director, so first, let me begin by giving you a tour of our facility, a brief history of our group, and what we're up against."

Thomas then showed them the enormous ultramodern underground facility, which was beneath a building in the center of the city. "This headquarters is a secret location that was supposed to be used as a nuclear fallout shelter and bunker for important military, government, and civilian personnel, but it never was. It has a primary energy-grid power source, state-of-the-art computers, a satellite, a radio, and tele-video communication equipment. We have hundreds of vetted, committed, and loyal personnel, who are experts in different fields and are needed to carry out our mission. Our location in the heart of a large, busy city permits us to enter and leave without arousing suspicion."

Ashlee stated, "This is very impressive. I never would have imagined something like this could exist."

Joe nodded in agreement and asked, "But why is this needed? What's the purpose of it?"

Thomas answered, "Good question. Let me fill you in. There is an ancient secret society called One World Order, which is embedded in all social spheres of all the countries in the world. They are evil and determined to have humanity destroy itself so that they can easily take over those who are left and establish a new world order, which can be controlled and manipulated at their will. They will stop at nothing to keep humanity from learning the truth of our origin and what's coming, which will decrease our chances for survival."

Ashlee said, "Well that sounds scary, but what truth and what's coming?"

Thomas continued, "Our founder, a very wealthy person in

our country, was approached many years ago by someone in One World Order for recruitment. After listening to what they wanted to accomplish and how, this person not only rejected them but also decided to fight back and stop them, using some of their same tactics. This person, our founder, became the first member of our Saving Earth Group. Since then, we've been known as SE Group or simply as the Group. Our founder and several other wealthy individuals provide us with vast financial resources and contacts worldwide for our fight."

Joe asked, "These contacts, are they civilians, in the military, government people, or what?"

Thomas replied, "We're a private organization but have unofficial support from many high government officials, military personnel, businesspeople, and local authorities throughout the world who are aware of the danger we're in. We only go by first names that we have chosen ourselves. Our recruitment is done in such a way that any given member only knows the immediate eight members of their cell and has only encrypted internet or computer contact with us, the main center cell and control."

Joe said, "That's what I call real contacts." They all laughed.

Thomas then said, "We stay in contact with our founder, who continues to monitor and direct our group but remains anonymous to all of us. This process is important in case anyone is captured because One World Order has made its mission to eliminate us a priority, as we are the only obstacle that can stop them. Our group has thousands of cells positioned in all levels of society and governments throughout the world; we even have assets within One World Order.

Joe asked, "Who are these people, and why do they want humanity's destruction?"

Thomas replied, "This is the greatest threat to the world. Most people are unaware of its presence and evil manipulations. Let me try to summarize what you're up against. I imagine that you have heard the biblical story of The Tower of Babel," he said.

Ashlee asked, "Well, yes, but what's that got to do with it?"

Thomas smiled grimly. "Everything you see, it started back then. Hundreds of thousands of years ago, an advanced civilization was established by super-evolved beings who came to Earth from another planet. Sumerians considered them gods and called them Anunnaki. They were here to mine for gold, which was just as rare where they came from and which they needed urgently to stabilize their world. They modified Earth to make it adaptable for survival, infusing their DNA into a local species to enhance their mental and physical abilities. They created the perfect creature for manual labor: the human being. This was a time when the gods walked among men, and advanced scientific knowledge was being taught to humanity so that humans could breed, learn to feed themselves, and survive against all other creatures and natural hazards."

"That sounds so incredible, almost science fiction," she stated.

"Yes," Thomas replied, "but I'm afraid it's real. Then war broke out among the gods over a dispute on how to deal with Earth and their creations—us. These beings had finished their work here, and they were returning to their place of origin. The question was what to do with their earthly creations. Some were in favor of letting us live and continue as we were—with all our mutations and imperfections. Some of this arose from gods breeding with human women, creating unique half-breeds known as Nephilim, demigods, or giants. The gods saw how quickly humans were evolving and learning. They feared that humanity could represent a danger in the future and decided to eliminate us by causing a worldwide flood cataclysm."

"Wow!" Ashlee exclaimed. Is this referring to the biblical story of the flood?"

Thomas nodded and continued. "Some gods favored helping humanity. They rebelled, but they lost, were exiled, and were known as fallen angels, but not before they warned us of what was to come so that we could prepare ourselves in order to survive. With their help, underground tunnels, caves, and boats were built throughout the world to shelter and carry thousands of men and animals. The gods, with their advanced technology, directed a huge asteroid toward Earth, which was starting to emerge from the ice age. The asteroid broke into thousands of pieces. This impacted North America, which was still covered with mile-thick glaciers from the ice age. With the force of millions of nuclear weapons, the tremendous impact caused an enormous fireball, which immediately melted the glaciers and caused ocean levels to rise hundreds of feet and worldwide flooding. With all the debris, dust, and ash in the atmosphere, this was followed by dropping temperatures and the continuation of the ice age, which lasted almost another thousand years."

Ashlee and Joe looked at each other, and then Joe said, "Did this really happen? How do we know?"

Thomas answered," Yes, it happened. This occurred approximately twelve thousand years ago. It's recorded in many cultures worldwide, such as Noah and the ark, the *Epic of Gilgamesh*, and the like. We survived, and as we emerged from the caves and tunnels, we proceeded to rebuild. With the teachings and knowledge that these beings had given us, we thrived and learned to work together to produce our food and rebuild cities such as Babel. It was then that a warrior king, Nimrod, son of Cush and grandson of Noah, decided that humanity would never again allow itself to be exterminated but would be equal to the gods who had created us."

Thomas went on explaining to Ashlee and Joe that this had been a time when humanity had built the first civilization, which had been united as one, and how King Nimrod of Babel had become a powerful leader and had ordered a tower built that would give them access to the gods. The watchers, who were agents of the gods and were left behind to monitor Earth until their return, alerted the gods. The gods tasked them to stop Nimrod and his men at all costs.

"Nimrod was killed, and the men were scattered to all regions of the Earth, sending humanity to a primitive beginning again. Upon Nimrod's death, he was revered by his pregnant widow, Semiramis, who claimed that her son Tammuz was, in reality, Nimrod reborn. Semiramis and her priests then invented many rituals to worship her as the mother of god and her son as a god." Thomas informed while Ashlee and Joe listened on with rapt attention. "Rituals, including mother-of-God worship, sunrise services, and the winter solstice festivals could be traced back to these pre-Christian times and ultimately to ancient Babylon. So thousands of years ago, the mother of all secret societies took root in One World Order. Its primary goal was reestablishing one government, one language, and one leader for all humanity so that they could challenge the gods upon their return."

Ashlee asked, "Is that what's coming?"

"Well, we believe that due to the increased activity from One World Order, the gods are returning. This secret society joined forces with none other than Lucifer himself and some of the fallen angels, and it has been under Satan's control since then. It, together with millions of misled, unwitting accomplice-followers, has become the most powerful secret society on the planet! And while many people continue to debate about secret organizations, the biggest secret organization thrives in plain sight. Satan along with Nimrod's secret society, One World Order, have persisted and thrived to this day. This Babylonian-type of system is the "mother of harlots," which has influenced all nations, governments, cultures, and world religions and which we were warned of in the Bible's book Revelations (Revelation 18:4)," Thomas shared solemnly.

Ashlee shook her head slowly. Her face was marked with an expression of disbelief. "Wow! I never imagined such a secret society like this could exist. So where do we fit in all of this?"

Thomas's visage returned to polite friendliness as he gave her a small smile before answering. "I will, but first, let me introduce some of our key members, who will explain it to you and help prepare you for your mission. They will give you all the details and answer your questions. Please follow me."

They went down a corridor and into the command center, a large room with many monitors and several people sitting at their stations. Thomas then started introducing the staff. "This is Mary. She's your computer expert. She can hack into any government, agency, or private computer system in the world."

Mary, a petite blonde-haired woman who had pink-tipped ends, gave them a wide smile and waved. "Hello. Welcome to our group."

Ashlee answered, "Nice to be here—we hope."

Thomas went ahead and introduced Peter, the electronic and communications expert, who could devise miniature weapons and advanced systems to communicate in any part of the world. He seemed like a quiet fellow, and other than a silent nod at them, he said nothing. He went back to work almost immediately.

Then there was Luke, the historian and expert in ancient civilizations and cultures. He gave a cheeky wink to Ashlee and a friendly grin to Joe. Bespectacled and wire-thin, Mathew was a religious expert, who was knowledgeable in Christianity, Judaism, Islam, Taoism, Buddhism, Hinduism, and many other religions worldwide. He seemed to be in a rush and murmured, "Hello," before rushing off.

"That's Mat for you; always in a rush." Thomas chuckled.

"John is our expert anthropologist and archeologist. Simon is one of the world's leading martial arts' experts and military tacticians. James is the coordinator for the command center and an expert in philosophy, the paranormal, mysticism, meditation, and all other extrasensory disciplines."

They welcomed them warmly, and then Mary said, "Welcome to our center."

Ashlee and Joe thanked everyone for their greetings. Thomas turned to both of them. "As you can see, we only go by first names— our given names or any others that you prefer. We don't share any other information that could identify us, but we do watch one another's back. With this, I'll leave you in good hands with your team, and they'll take over where I left off. See you later."

After Thomas left, James approached Joe and Ashlee with a friendly grin. "I'm sure you have a thousand questions, but let's get you settled in for now. You've had a long day, and tomorrow, we'll start bright and early with your training and fill you in on all the rest. Follow me, and I'll take you to your living quarters, which will be your homes from now on. Don't worry, you won't be disappointed."

James headed out the door, and Joe and Ashlee followed him. He led them to a hallway, which resembled a luxury hotel corridor, before he stopped in front of a door. He turned to Ashlee. "This is your apartment. It's been programmed with your DNA. Stand within two feet of the entry, and it will scan you automatically and open to let you in. Anyone else wanting to enter has to announce themselves and wait for you to command the door to open."

Ashlee approached the door. It opened soundlessly. A soft and pleasant female voice said, "Hello, Ashlee. Welcome home. I'm Mia, the group's AI computer system. You can access me from anywhere. I can display things on a screen or project holographic images. I can assist you with data and can control lights, appliances, audio-videos of your choice, temperature, or anything else you desire."

When Ashlee entered, the lights turned on, and soft music started playing. She observed that it was a beautifully decorated apartment and was spacious. It had a warm feel to it. Ashlee said, "Hi! Mia, it's nice being here."

A holographic image of Mia asked, "Can I get you something to eat or prepare you a warm bath?"

"Whoa! This is some cool *Back to the Future* kind of stuff. I'm going to like being here very much," she said while smiling at Joe. The men chuckled at her. She turned and waved goodnight before the door shut behind her.

"Come on. Yours is down the hall." James led Joe to his quarters before bidding him goodnight and taking his leave.

★★★

Joe entered his apartment and found it to be almost strikingly identical to the prior apartment that he had lived in, in Manhattan. This left him feeling bewildered. Mia then said, "Hi, Joe. Welcome to your new home. I hope everything meets with your approval?"

Joe replied, "Hi, Mia. Yes, it's very warming to see a familiar place. How did you do this? How did you know what my apartment looked like?"

"It wasn't difficult. I can access all your past expenditures and purchases, including video recordings from your apartment that various electronic devices had taken. I wanted you to feel at home, but of course, you have an upgrade of all your appliances and communication and entertainment devices. You also have an incredibly advanced and superfast computer system at your disposal."

Joe said, "Thank you, Mia. That was very thoughtful of you. Yes, you have my approval, and I feel very much at home." With this, Mia wished him goodnight.

CHAPTER SEVEN

THE TRAINING

"**G**ood morning, Ashlee," Mia said as soon as Ashlee woke up. Her volume was soft and soothing to Ashlee's ears. "May I bring breakfast to you, or would you prefer to eat in the dining hall?"

Ashlee smiled and sat up. She stretched leisurely before letting out a sigh. "Good morning, Mia. I would like to eat in and then take a shower if that's OK?"

"I'll order your favorite for you. Simon will meet you at the command center afterward," Mia promptly replied before turning quiet.

Once they were dressed and ready, Joe and Ashlee arrived at the command room. Everyone was already at his or her post working. They looked up upon their arrival. Joe greeted them on both of their behalves. "Good morning, everyone. We're here, so what's next?"

Simon stood up and answered, "This morning, you're with me. I'm going to help you improve your fighting skills."

Ashlee replied, "OK, but is this necessary?"

Simon looked at Joe and Ashlee and answered," Your lives will depend on it."

Joe turned to Ashlee, nodded, and said, "Well since you put it that way, lead the way."

They followed Simon to another facility section, where they had a complete gymnasium setup. "Wow!" they both exclaimed.

"This is very impressive," Ashlee mumbled while looking around.

"OK." Simon rubbed his palms together. "Let's see what you both can do. Go ahead and attack me so I can gauge your skills," he said as he took a wider stance.

Joe frowned uncertainly. "Are you sure? We have been practicing, and we have achieved a great degree of coordination to trounce an opponent."

Simon nodded calmly. "Yes, show me your moves."

With this, Joe and Ashlee attacked Simon, but despite their coordinated moves and speed, they could not defeat Simon. After a few minutes and having tried everything they knew, they finally gave up.

Ashlee stood with her hands on her hips, panting lightly. A fine sheen of sweat was on her forehead. "We did everything we could to defeat you, but we failed. I have never seen anyone with your level of skills. I don't believe we can beat you." Joe nodded while catching his breath.

"Well," Simon said, looking as unruffled as he had before their fight, "we have a big problem because if you can't defeat me, you'll surely lose—possibly your lives—when you go up against your new enemy. Unfortunately, I'm not skillful enough to defeat them; they are at a level way above me."

Both stared at him, flabbergasted. Joe asked, "What enemy, and how can we possibly defeat them if we already showed you all we got?"

Simon clapped his hands once on his thighs before rubbing his palms on his sweats. "I'll let Thomas go over who you're going up against, but I can tell you that they are very skillful. However, they can surely be defeated if you practice and follow my instructions. You see, up till now, you have been coordinating your thoughts and movements in real time, reacting, and adjusting to your opponent. The moves during a confrontation are selected after our mind first calculates and extrapolates all the possible outcomes. The most likely move to succeed is selected and sent to the motor centers so that it can send the signal to the appropriate muscle groups to accomplish it."

"This is done at incredibly high speeds, especially if you have years of practice. Well, if you can both focus your mind's power on your opponent and tap into that thought process, you can detect his next move before his motor cortex has a chance to act. You will be ahead of your opponent by fractions of a millisecond, which is enough to give you the advantage needed to win, unless you're confronting someone with the same ability. Then it would come down to who can influence the thoughts of the other and cause the other one to make the wrong move. I'm betting on you two, so what do you say?"

Ashlee was amazed and very impressed with Simon's knowledge of martial arts and the mind's ability. She sensed that Joe felt the same way, so she nodded while saying, "Yes, we'll follow your instructions and practice with our bodies and our minds."

Simon smiled widely. "Great. Let's practice some more, and afterward, you'll go back to the command room; Thomas will be waiting for you."

After the morning session, Joe and Ashlee returned to the command room. There, the rest of the team was at their stations working, including Thomas, who upon seeing them, got up and approached them. "Good. You're back. How was your time with Simon?"

"Incredible," Ashlee answered.

Joe shook his head slowly. "Definitely an experience. We didn't realize there was a whole different level of martial arts that combined mind and body until Simon showed us," Joe elaborated.

Thomas chuckled. "You will find that we have advanced equipment and techniques, which you won't find anywhere else in the world. We will use them to prepare and train you, converting you into one of our most critical elements for our mission's success and Earth's future. One World Order is already aware of your existence, and it's their priority to stop you at all costs. Their agents will be constantly on the lookout for you both, with orders to eliminate you onsite."

"OK," said Ashley. "But why us, how did you find us, and what's our role in all of this?"

"Well," Thomas said, "first, let me tell you a story about a humble priest in South America, and then it will become clear to you. Carlo Crespi was born in Legnano, Italy, on May 29, 1891, to a local farmworker and his wife. In 1907, he began his novitiate in Foglizzo, and between 1909 and 1911, he studied philosophy in Valsalice. On Sunday, January

28, 1917, he was ordained a priest. He was a Salesian monk. In 1921, Crespi graduated in natural sciences with a specialization in botany from the University of Padua. After three months, he also graduated in piano and composition from the Cesare Pollini Conservatory in Padua.

"He was a person of many talents—an educator, botanist, anthropologist, musician, and above all, humanitarian. He is in the process of beatification by the Catholic Church. Father Carlos Crespi Croci dedicated his life to worship and charity and lived in the small town of Cuenca in Ecuador for more than fifty years. Because of his missionary work, he became close to the indigenous people of the Ecuadorian Amazon. He was a highly respected person among the tribes, who considered him a true friend of theirs.

Ashlee said, "Great! He was a wonderful priest, but what does it have to do with all of this?"

Thomas laughed and said, "Everything. Let me explain. The indigenous people gave Father Crespi gifts of ancient artifacts to thank him for his work and for helping them. They said that the items brought to him had been found in subterranean tunnels and caves in the jungles of Ecuador, which span more than two hundred kilometers, starting from the village of Cuenca. The indigenous people considered them sacred, so the tunnel locations were never revealed, not even to Father Crespi. They are still unknown. Many were killed by the indigenous people in their search for the mysterious subterranean tunnels with the hidden treasure."

Joe asked, "So this is a treasure hunt?"

"Not quite," replied Thomas. "You see, the amazing artifacts given to him had uncanny similarities with civilizations of the East. There were enough of them to fill up a large museum. The Vatican trusted Father Crespi to open a museum in the Salesian school at Cuenca. Up until 1960, it was the largest museum in Ecuador. However, Father Crespi, who was recognized as an archaeological authority, tried contacting archaeologists, historians, government agencies, etc., and told them that most of the symbols and prehistoric representations on the artifacts were older than the flood. He insisted that he could prove that there was a direct connection between the Old World

(Babylon-Sumeria) and the New World (pre-Inca civilizations). No one was interested in his theories. He was ridiculed. This had always been an embarrassment for the Vatican because it went against mainstream opinions."

Ashlee stated, "Well it does sound farfetched."

Thomas replied, "Yes, it does. The whole issue probably would have been forgotten if not for the fact that one night, the museum was burned down, and it was no accident. We realized someone was trying to destroy the evidence and truth of their origins. This is why we got involved. Most of the artifacts were destroyed, except or a few that Father Crespi managed to save. We believe One World Order burned the museum down on July 20, 1962. When Father Crespi died, all the remaining artifacts that he had kept in a room next to his sleeping quarters and hidden from public view disappeared forever. Rumors suggested that the artifacts were shipped to the Vatican or that the Ecuadoran government or local authorities took them. But they're not true; we have them."

Ashlee said, "Wow! That's an amazing story."

Thomas continued talking. "Father Crespi died in 1982, thinking that no one believed in his findings, but we did. The moment Father Crespi died, we had our members in Cuenca secure the artifacts. They were secretly brought here. They consisted of a number of gold metal sheets covered with graphic characters, which may be some kind of ancient writing—probably the oldest ever known in the world! One of the golden metal sheets is subdivided into fifty-six squares. Each one is filled with a different graphic character, and our experts have been working on deciphering them. Others were replete with engravings of animals such as elephants, snakes, jaguars, and wild beasts of every kind. There were images of a horse-drawn chariot clearly etched into metal, resembling an Egyptian chariot."

"Very interesting story." Joe folded his arms across his chest and had a skeptical look on his face. "But you haven't answered our questions."

Thomas continued. "Our experts were able to decipher a small portion, which was enough to confirm what I told you before—that beings called the Anunnaki came to Earth hundreds of thousands of years ago. They were an advanced humanoid, extraterrestrial species from another planet, who constructed bases of operations to mine gold after discovering that our planet was rich in the precious metal they needed for their survival back on their planet. The Anunnaki hybridized their species and Homo erectus via in vitro fertilization in order to create us humans as slave species of miners."

Ashlee with a look of amazement exclaimed, "Oh! So we were created to be slaves, and there's life out there in the universe and aliens."

Thomas replied, "Yes, but that's not all of it. When they were finished mining and ready to leave, they decided to eliminate us because they were concerned that we could pose a future danger to them. Some didn't agree. There was a rebellion among them, and some stayed behind to help us. They warned us that a worldwide flood was coming followed by freezing temperatures that would last hundreds and maybe thousands of years. The Anunnaki, or gods as the humans were calling them, helped us build boats to evacuate those in low-lying areas and to create tunnels and caves in the higher altitudes as underground shelters for the protection of the survivors and to store knowledge that humans would need afterward to rebuild and repopulate the earth."

Perplexed, Joe asked, "So some of these so-called gods helped us to survive a world catastrophe that they caused?"

Thomas said, "Yes, and we should be grateful because the ones who stayed behind to help us were exiled from their own people for doing so. Approximately twelve thousand years ago, the flood came, followed by a resurgence of an ice age, which also destroyed the Anunnaki bases on Earth. We know these shelters were all over the world, but we only had the coordinates of the one near Göbekli Tepe. Five years ago, we sent a cargo ship to the Mediterranean Sea with two helicopters on board. When we were near the coast of southern Turkey's border with Syria, which is a dangerous war zone, we flew low, evaded radars, and made it to the target site east of Göbekli Tepe, a cave on a hillside just south of the town of Ortaoren.

"We started digging, found the entrance, and then opened it. What we found was amazing: broken pieces of pottery, a piece of a possible flat stone tablet, stone statues, hundreds of sheets of gold, silver, and other metals with engravings, and flat, round quartz crystal tablets also with engravings. That cave seemed to have been the final resting place of one of the gods who had stayed behind to help. There was an image on the wall showing a large body lying on a stone slab at least twelve-to-fifteen feet long, and an image of smaller men standing next to it, as if in prayer.

"We loaded everything into the helicopters, documented and photographed the wall images, sealed the cave, and left. Since then, our people have been working to decipher the engravings. They are a very ancient type of language, a mixture of hieroglyphs and cuneiform characters, which are similar to Egyptian and Sumerian but different. We've made a few advances; we learned that only a few of the gods who rebelled and stayed behind decided to help us. The rest only wanted to use us to get revenge on the gods who had abandoned them."

Ashlee asked, "What happened to these beings?"

Thomas chuckled and answered, "Well, that's one of the reasons you and Joe are here. Those beings didn't live forever. Their bodies decayed after hundreds of years, but their souls or inner energy DNA is immortal. It was passed on a little bit at a time when they bred with human women, who then passed it on through their X chromosomes. Generations or thousands of years later under specific circumstances, if two humans have a large amount each of DNA remnants from the same alien being, it can recombine itself in the offspring, who would acquire some of the features of the original being or could totally reincarnate.

"Also, when two humans have enough DNA in each of them from the same original being, and they are able to share their energies, they can release energy spikes or surges when they are together. These energy spikes can be detected with the right equipment, and that's what we were monitoring when we detected yours. We have a long way to go in deciphering the data, but we do know that the gods are coming back. Some alien beings or so-called fallen who were angels left behind want revenge, and they plan to challenge them upon arrival. They are preparing for it using the One World Order society. They want humankind to join in their quest. So you see, Ashlee, that answers your other question of why you?"

"Oh, my god," she exclaimed, "it's unbelievable. So we have alien DNA that gives us certain abilities, and we're in the middle of a battle between good and evil?"

Thomas replied, "Yes, and if we don't get help stopping the OWO, and they challenge the gods, who knows what Earth and humankind's fate will be."

Joe looked concern then asked, "So where do we start?"

Thomas replied, "Well, first, we need to find the beings who helped us before to see if they can help us again with what's coming. That's where you come in. You both have DNA from the same alien being, Anunnaki or the fallen angel. It seems you both have ancient DNA linked to an ancient people, who were inhabitants of the United States Southwest. They were known as the ancient ones and ancestors of the Hohokam, Puebloan, or Anasazi. They were originally from South America, Mesoamerica, and southern Mexico. They migrated north to the American Southwest of Arizona, Colorado, Utah, and New Mexico. They were much older people than the Clovis culture of northern and midwestern North America. These ancient ones are the ancestors of modern native tribes such as the Hopi, Paiute, Pima, Tarahumaran, and Aztecan (aka Nahuatl). After the cataclysm during which the Clovis culture was wiped out in addition to the flora and fauna of North America, the only survivors were the ancient ones of the southwest."

"OK," said Ashlee. "So we are descendants of these ancient ones. Is that it?"

"Yes," answered Thomas. "But you also have the DNA of the Anunnaki god, which helped them survive. He helped them hide underground for many generations. When the earth's surface became safe again, he helped them rebuild and taught them agriculture and the way to survive. He was not immortal, but his DNA was. In agreement with the ancient ones, it was decided that his DNA be passed on to preserve it. The ancient ones selected some of their young, who were healthy, strong women, to breed with the Anunnaki god since his DNA could only be linked to the X chromosome. In this way, he was preserved forever. When enough of his DNA is recombined, his abilities will manifest themselves again. Well, both of your mothers are descendants of these young women. After seven continuous generations of increased X-chromosome accumulation of the same being's DNA, it gives you enough alien DNA to access his abilities. When you combine your energies, this being is able to remember some of its past."

Ashlee was speechless. Her mind raced to make sense of it all. She could sense that Joe was in awe and was undergoing the same thought process. She looked at Joe who had a confused expression.

Joe held up a palm and then said, "So let me get this straight. We have alien DNA of a being who could help us save Earth. But we don't know how the saving bit will come to fruition. We also need to be careful so that we don't get killed by some fanatical group first. Does that about sum it up?"

Thomas nodded. "Yes, that's about it."

Ashlee asked, "So how do we proceed from here?"

Thomas replied, "We would like to send you to the right locations on Earth, where energy concentrations or other secret storage sites are. There, you'll be able to expose this being to it. Then through increased awareness and enlightenment, maybe he can regain his memories and abilities, which will hopefully help us survive."

"No pressure," Joe said, throwing up his hands before dropping them. He then looked at Ashlee and smiled. "I'm in. What about you?"

Ashlee grinned back and answered, "Me too." She was thinking about how unbelievable everything happening was, but she knew this is what she was meant to do. "So yes, I'm to the end. What's next?"

Thomas then clapped his hands once and exclaimed, "Great! You will continue your martial arts' training in the mornings with Simon, and in the afternoons, you'll train with James. He will help you improve your meditation and special abilities, some of which you already know, and some of the new ones you'll learn. You will also receive tech devices and weapons we have custom made for you. You'll be sent on your first field mission when you are ready. Do you have any questions?" They both said that they didn't. "OK then, go with James and try to learn from him."

Ashlee and Joe followed James to a comfortable room with a warm feeling and dim lights. There was no furniture but only thick floor mats. James said, "This is our meditation room. Please sit. I have read your files and have a pretty good idea of your level of ability as individuals and together. I'm going to guide you into how to meditate individually to enhance your personal abilities, combine your DNAs, and help awaken the light being you have within you. Remember, you are unique because you have more traces of an ancient being's DNA than the ordinary person does.

"You have to let it help you increase your inner energy to increase your personal abilities, such as thought projection, mind reading, aura perception, telekinesis, telepathy, and increasing your body healing, strength, speed, and tolerance. So let's start from the basics. As you know, meditation is a form of balancing, healing, and raising one's frequency to give your body commands or to receive messages from higher energy planes. Messages can be in thought form and can be experienced by any of the five senses or the intuitive area of the mind. During meditation, you may feel motion or pressure in your chakra energy centers because you absorb and build internal energy. Don't let it worry you; it is completely normal. Do you have any questions?" Both Ashlee and Joe shook their heads.

"OK, we'll start with individual meditation. First of all, I want you find a comfortable position. You can either sit or lie down. Then inhale slowly through your nose and hold your breath as comfortably as possible. Exhale slowly through your mouth. Repeat two more times or as is comfortable for you. Relax your body, starting with your toes and then going to your feet, legs, back, arms, shoulders, neck, and head. Then decide where to go while meditating or just concentrate on blanking your mind. Once you have achieved total relaxation, try connecting with the astral plane and cosmic energy surrounding us."

As Ashlee was following James's instructions, she felt her body gradually relax to the point where she felt weightless. She could sense that Joe was experiencing the same thing. Gradually, her mind became a blank screen, and she could feel energy flowing through her.

James continued, "Your bodies are vibrating matter and energy; it is the same. So now I want you to use that energy to create a plasma ball of energy between your hands. Start by placing your elbows close to your body. Now place the palms of your hands facing each other, between one and two inches apart but not touching. Rotate your hands slowly in small circles; your dominant hand may move faster or make larger circles. You should start feeling a pull between your hands; this is the human energy or auric field. Rotate your hands faster as you feel the energies build up."

Ashlee started to feel the energy building up between her hands. She could also sense Joe's energy build up, which was more intense than hers.

James then said, "You are building a plasma ball of energy. When you stop moving your hands, hold them in a cupped position. You should be able to feel the plasma ball. You can use it any way you want. To heal your body, build up energy inside yourself by placing it in one of your chakras or heal another person with the palms of your hands. Everything is energy. In physical terms, we live and move in an eternal, infinite system of energies and forces, which compose our universe. The intensity of the energy created between your hands varies. Sometimes, there will be little energy transferred, but other times, the effect of using this plasma ball can really be intense."

"Wow! This is amazing," exclaimed Joe. "What else can we do with it?"

James chuckled and said, "I've seen people take the ball and throw it across a room, moving objects. I believe that you both will be able to do way more. To avoid unpleasant shocks, after you finish, ground yourself by placing your hands flat on the floor or touch a wall. Once you have mastered today's lesson, when you meditate, try practicing your other abilities such as thought projection, mind reading, aura perception, telekinesis, and telepathy, along with increasing your body's healing power, strength, speed, and tolerance. I know you have these abilities; you just need to learn to increase their intensity. Practice daily, and when I see that you're ready, I will show you what you can do together, OK?"

"OK," they replied. James bid them goodbye. Then he left so that they could continue practicing.

CHAPTER EIGHT

KOKABIEL

A shlee and Joe continued their daily practice routine: martial arts in the morning with Simon, whom they could now defeat with relative ease, and meditation in the afternoons. In between sessions, the other team members filled them in on the information they had gathered up to that point. Luke brought them up to speed on ancient civilizations and cultures, which were mainly Egyptian, Sumerian, and Babylonian ones, and how they related to the Anunnaki or the old gods. John reviewed ancient dwellings, ruins, and energy centers on Earth, which could be important in helping them, locate other hidden relics or treasure troves of knowledge.

Mathew gave lectures on humans' origin and purpose in life from the viewpoint of different religions and the reason there are forces trying to stop and destroy them. Of course, all of this was to help them figure out what they needed to do to fight for their survival.

Their meditation practice paid off. They became proficient at mind reading, aura perception, increasing their healing abilities, strength, speed, and tolerance. Ashlee was exceptionally skilled at thought projection and telekinesis. Joe was good at throwing plasma balls with deadly accuracy. They had excellent telepathy with each other, which was somewhat limited with others. They realized the importance of the work done by everyone at the center and of their roles. They were very impressed with the state-of-the-art facility and technological advances, which they learned were part alien—built from the information retrieved from the caves in Ecuador and Turkey.

One day as Joe and Ashlee were practicing their daily meditation, James walked in. "You both have great abilities, and I'm very pleased with your progress. But today, I'm going to show you what you can do if you combine your energies during meditation. I know that once before, you had this experience; that's how we detected your energy surge and found you. By the way, you don't have to worry about being detected here. This whole facility is shielded."

"Great!" Ashlee said as she stood up with Joe. "We were wondering when we were going to try it again. It was such an intense experience, and it felt like we were each a different person yet simultaneously both of us."

"That's correct," James agreed with a smile. "It was because you were a different being during that experience. Let me explain to you as best as I can. We learned this from the relics we recovered. You can get additional information from the rest of our team. Humans were created hundreds of thousands of years ago by the ancient gods using some of their DNA to enhance the existing Homo erectus species so that they could be their workforce. But after the rebellion and war among the gods over a disagreement on what to do with us once they had finished their stay here on Earth, the rebels lost, and they were left behind on Earth to also perish during the global cataclysm they were going to cause.

"Some of the fallen gods or angels, as they are more commonly referred to, decided to help us survive. In the months that followed before the end of the world, they helped build shelters and lived among us after the cataclysm for a thousand years. They were able to live many thousands of years but were not immortal. Their bodies decayed, but their energy was able to live in the DNA that they transferred during breeding with human women. Some of these fallen angels ultimately passed on their entire DNA, which was spread among their offspring. They knew that it would survive through thousands of years and generations. It could recombine when enough of it was brought together again. Since it was passed only in the X chromosomes, someone would need at least 50 percent alien DNA to start the recombination. This was achieved if the female came from a line of women who had been acquiring alien DNA of the same specific being for at least seven generations without interruptions.

"But even if the entire X chromosome is alien, it's not more than 40 percent, which is the maximum it can hold. So you need another human with an X chromosome who has at least 10 percent or more of the same specific alien DNA and who can share it with you. It just so happens that you both are on the same frequency and can combine your energies. You're balance partners. But also, you each have approximately 40 percent alien DNA of the same specific being in your X chromosomes, which has been keeping in contact with itself over past lives and thousands of years in order to bring you together to recombine, so you're also soulmates. The odds of this happening are astronomical, making you two unique and valuable."

"Whoa!" Joe shook his head incredulously. His eyes were wide in awe as he exhaled loudly. "I knew we connected, but I didn't realize how deep it was."

"Yes," Ashley agreed. Marvel was clearly in her tone. "I now understand why I feel more complete but different when we're close to each other."

James nodded. "Exactly, when you merge, the alien DNA recombines, and the being awakes and comes back to life while you're in meditation, so you are different but simultaneously the same. We learned this from deciphering some of the writings from the cave in Turkey. When the genetic material from these ancient gods is recombined, they are able to acquire an energy form or an astral body, and they can travel in the astral plane. Also, during astral projection, your conscious mind leaves your physical body and moves into the astral body. Still, you remain attached to your physical body by a silver umbilical type cord. Some see the cord, and others do not. You are aware of your surroundings and everything happening while out of your body, but the alien being is too. It is not only awake but in control."

Ashlee frowned with a hint of concern. "Is it safe to let it come back to life? I know it's been guiding our lives so that we would meet and then let it recombine, but is it good or evil?"

Joe patted her shoulder reassuringly. "I can't tell you how or why, but I have this feeling that it's not only good but that it also wants to help us in our mission."

"You're right, Joe," James said, smiling at him before turning to Ashlee. "This particular being helped the humans once they resurfaced from their shelters after the cataclysm. It helped humankind rebuild and taught it agriculture, astronomy, mathematics, and other knowledge that it needed to survive."

"But how do you know this?" Ashlee inquired.

"These beings left recordings on stone, flat, round quartz discs, and gold and silver sheets that they knew would withstand the ravages of time. They knew we would find them one day, so they left us with knowledge and instructions to help us rebuild and understand what happened. This included instructions on how to build the monitoring device we used to find you and what to do. This being left us a record of his DNA so that we could identify it when we came across it, and we did—in both of you. His name was or is Kokabiel. He was a good being in spite of being a fallen angel. His name means star of God," he explained.

There was a moment of silence before Joe and Ashlee expressed their wonderment and willingness to jump headfirst into it. Ashlee looked at Joe, who was nodding, and exclaimed, "Wow! We're in. What do we do next?"

"OK." James rubbed his hands in clear anticipation. "You are both star gatekeepers, which means you have specific genetic codes that give you the ability to not only increase the vibration of other souls but also to activate dormant DNA, which allows those souls to enter into a different dimension, such as the astral plane. You must first find a comfortable spot, as the physical body sometimes gets cold when you travel out. You then sit back-to-back, holding each other's hands to close the circuit. Your right hand holds your partner's left hand and vice versa. You start with meditation. Once you both have achieved total relaxation, your bodies are asleep, but your minds are awake, focus on creating an opening above your heads. Let go of the fear of leaving your physical body. See yourselves floating away and use your minds to lift out of your physical bodies and pass through the gate above your heads that you created. You may feel a release or perhaps hear a sound as your conscious selves separate and leave your bodies, which means that your astral projection is successful.

"Keep the sessions to under an hour as the silver cord connects your body and the invisible force. Use this to guide your consciousness back to your physical body. Once you're in the astral plane, there will be only one astral body. Kokabiel will be in charge, but the consciousness of all three of you will be in there. Kokabiel will direct what the astral body does and where it goes, but you will be linked in thought with each other. To end the session, you both need to pull on the silver cord until you are back to your physical body. Even Kokabiel can't stop you. So you will learn to work together for the good of the earth and humankind. OK, any questions?"

"No, we're good," Joe quickly answered, and Ashlee nodded.

"Right then," James clapped his hands once, giving them each a look of anticipation, "give it a try."

★★★

They sat on the floor, back-to-back and linked their hands as they were instructed. Joe entered a state of total meditation and relaxation. It was very quiet, and he felt weightless as if he were floating. He didn't hear or feel anything of his surroundings, with one exception; he could sense and almost feel Ashlee, and he was aware of her thoughts as if they were linked. He focused on creating an energy opening above their heads, mentally asking Ashlee to do the same. Suddenly, there was a loud thunderous noise and bright lights. Then he found himself in an astral body of pure energy. It was a weird feeling, but he was aware that both he and Ashlee were linked in thought and astral body.

"Oh my God!" Ashlee exclaimed. "This is amazing. Joe, it really is incredible."

Suddenly, they heard a voice that was so vague it felt like a thought.

"It's nice to be able to finally communicate with you both. I have been with you for thousands of years, trying to guide you to this very moment."

"Nice to meet you too. Who are you?" Joe questioned.

The entity seemed to hesitate before replying. "I'm not sure. My memories seem to be fragmented, but I know I've existed for eons. Do you know me?"

"Well, sort of," answered Ashlee. "We know that you left us information over twelve thousand years ago to help us rebuild after a worldwide destructive event at that time. You also stated your name to be Kokabiel. Does it sound familiar to you?" she inquired.

"Somewhat. I seem to have fragmented images of my past, but it's still unclear," answered Kokabiel. Joe and Ashlee then gave Kokabiel a rundown of everything they knew and what the team members had told them.

"So as you can see, we're hoping that by exposing you to the locations we know have importance or to energy centers, you may be able to restore your memories so that you can help us, as you once did before, to save the earth," said Ashlee.

"Yes, I believe that's a good plan. We should try it," replied Kokabiel.

"Great!" Joe said. "First, can I call you Koka? Your name's too long. Are we really talking, or is it telepathy?"

"It's more like thought sharing; we're in one another's minds. Yes, you can call me Koka," he answered, chuckling. "So in this astral body, we'll be able to navigate in the astral plane, access places, view a parallel reality, visit another planet or dimension, meet other angels, do things you couldn't on your own, and tap into knowledge and energies that can help restore me so that I can help you save mankind, and I'll be in control?" Koka asked.

"Yes, Koka," Ashlee said, laughing. "But don't forget; only we can pull on the silver cord whenever we want and end the trip. This reminds me, it's time to go back."

"OK," he answered, "let's call it a day." With this, Joe and Ashlee pulled on the silver cord, and they were instantly back in their bodies and very happy with the experience and meeting Koka.

ANUNNAKI

"So what did you think of your experience and meeting our fallen angel friend?" asked Thomas, who was in the meditation room with James and the rest of the team. They had been waiting anxiously for Ashlee and Joe to return to their bodies and to give them a rundown of their experience.

"It was incredible," Joe replied.

Ashlee then said, "There are no words to describe what we felt and saw. We were floating in this ocean of energy with thousands, maybe millions, of brilliant light points. We could see and hear the sounds from the physical world but from another dimension. It felt invigorating and as if the world was within our reach."

Joe nodded in agreement and then added, "As for Kokabiel or Koka, as I like to call him, he's our friend; no doubt about it. It was amazing being able to communicate with a being that's been around for thousands of years. Unfortunately, at this time, he's not much help. His memories and knowledge are fragmented, but he's willing to do whatever's necessary to help us."

Thomas grinned. He was clearly ecstatic about this development. "Excellent, that's what we were hoping for. We have now confirmed the findings from the caves that beings visited us in ancient times— gods, fallen angels, or any other name you like. We know that some helped us like Koka, so we have to get him to help us again."

Everyone agreed, and then Mathew, who had a worried look, asked, "So what's next? How do we convince the world that we are going to be revisited? We don't know if that's good or bad for us. How do we stop One World Order from taking over and challenging god?"

CHAPTER NINE

THE START

O nce the whole team was back at the control room, Thomas finally answered. He seemed to sober at the severity of the situation. "We need to help restore Koka by exposing him to ancient sites for knowledge and to high energy flow centers. That means sending Ashlee and Joe into the field as soon as we can get them ready."

"You're right. Mary and I will search for sites. With my help and her computer skills, we'll hopefully find a good location and coordinates for you," John offered.

"Their martial arts' training is complete," Simon informed them, folding his arms.

"Also, they are now experts in meditation, and their psychic abilities are impressive," stated James with a smirk.

"Good. What about you, Peter? What do you have for us?" asked Thomas.

"I have implantable microchip communicators, which we built using ancient alien instructions, and personally activated energy weapons for them. So if you are done with them, I would like to take them to my lab," replied Peter, glancing from Thomas to Joe and Ashlee.

"Sounds good, Peter. OK, let's get to work, everyone. James, you coordinate everything. Let me know when you're ready for the first field mission and what you'll need," Thomas ordered.

Ashlee and Joe followed Peter to the lab, which was in a large compound area that was well-equipped. Peter showed them a very tiny microchip and explained that it was a powerful two-way communication, listening device and GPS tracker.

"These will be inserted into an air cell in your left mastoid bone behind the ear. It will be protected and almost completely indestructible, no matter what you do or what you're exposed to. It's activated as soon as it's inserted, and it will keep you in continuous contact with the center no matter where you are. Also, these microchips are constantly monitored by Mia. You can deactivate or activate them by ordering Mia to do so in case you need privacy. Do you have any questions?" Peter raised a questioning brow.

"Only one. Will it hurt when you insert it?" Joe inquired with a frightened look. Ashlee and Peter laughed. Joe rubbed the back of his neck sheepishly as his ears turned red from embarrassment.

"No, it's painless. I will insert them using a very fine needle and trocar, which injects fast-acting local anesthetic. It takes maybe five seconds, and then it's all over."

Joe gave a sigh of relief and said, "Good."

Ashlee shook her head at him amusedly. Then she turned to Peter with a raised brow. "How do we know these chips are safe?"

Peter grinned. "We know from what we've learned so far that they were using this technology themselves. We assume that they want to help and not hurt us. Of course, we can't be 100 percent sure until we try them, but we'll find out very soon, don't you think?"

Joe and Ashlee looked at each other and smiled. Ashlee then said, "Great! Let's find out."

Peter went ahead and proceeded to insert the microchip in Ashlee and then in Joe. It just took a few seconds. "Are you OK?"

"Yes," they replied and smiled.

Peter then explained the unique weapon that had been developed just for them. It was a bracelet that looked like a watch. "This is a potent weapon that we developed from the instructions left for us. It goes on your wrist—preferably the left—and it is mind controlled with the help of the microchip in your head and Mia. This bracelet absorbs the energy that surrounds us and accumulates it. Extending your arm and hand will fire a devastating beam of energy at wherever or whatever you're pointing at. It will automatically recharge itself, and you can control the energy beam's intensity to destroy or stun. All you have to do is think it, and Mia will carry it out. The bracelet is coded with your DNA, so no one else can use it. It can't be removed unless you give Mia the command to release it. Do you have any questions?" Peter inquired.

"Wow!" exclaimed Joe. "Incredible. Can we try them out?"

"Sure. Let me show you where our indoor range is, and you can practice target shooting until you feel confident in using them. By the way, they are water, heat, cold, and shockproof, so that you never have to remove them unless you want to," replied Peter.

Once they were at the indoor range, Peter said, "OK, Joe, you go first. See that bull's-eye target back there? I want you to try and hit it with a low intensity beam."

As he aimed his arm toward the target, Joe replied, "No problem." Suddenly, there was a loud noise with an intense flash of light and an explosion. As the smoke dissipated, it was obvious that the target was completely destroyed. Joe looked very surprised and stated, "Oops! I think it was just a bit too intense."

Ashley laughed, saying, "You think?"

Smiling, Peter said, "OK, you two. Stay here and practice until your thoughts and actions are completely synchronized, and you have achieved complete control of your bracelets' power."

Back at the command center, Mary, John, Luke, and Mathew had been working for days trying to determine where to send Ashlee and Joe on their first mission. Determining what energy center or ancient site they should send them to had been very frustrating, to say the least. They knew that once Ashlee and Joe left the center's protection, they would be able to be detected by One World agents and subject to attacks.

Finally, Mathew turned to Mary, Luke, and John. Sounding very excited, he blurted out, "That's it; I've got it! OK, everyone, it's time for a meeting. Call Thomas, Simon, James, Peter, Ashlee, and Joe."

Once everyone was at the command center, James looked at Thomas and said, "We found our site."

"Great," said Thomas. "Let's hear it."

"Mount Hermon," answered Mathew, "and back to where it all started."

Joe frowned. "Are you sure? I don't know of any ancient ruins at that location."

"You're right, but what we need is an energy center so that Koka can regain his full potential; that way, it will be easier for him to restore his memories," Luke explained.

"That's correct." Mathew looked from Luke to Joe. "You see, in the book of Enoch, Mount Hermon is the place where the watcher class of fallen angels descended to Earth after they were expelled."

"That location's on a ley line at the thirty-third parallel with a high energy concentration that our visitors were able to use to establish a landing site," James informed them.

"How do we know if it's still effective? Those visitations happened over twelve thousand years ago in ancient times." Ashlee folded her arms and pursed her lips.

"True." Mathew nodded. "But it wasn't the last time someone used this energy. Do you recall in your religious education reading about the transfiguration of Jesus Christ, which was witnessed by his disciples Peter, James, and John?"

"I believe that happened at Mount Tabor, didn't it?" Joe tilted his head contemplatively.

"Not quite," replied Mathew. "It's true that according to church tradition, the event took place on Mount Tabor, but after some research, we discovered that it's not really where it happened. All documented writings of this event, including the gospels of Mark, Matthew, and Luke, never mentioned the name of the mount. They only state that Jesus asked his disciples to wait while he went up the mount accompanied by Peter, James, and John. There, they witnessed Moses and Elijah appearing and Jesus being transfigured. His face and clothes became dazzlingly bright. Just before this, Jesus had been at Caesarea Philippi, which was near the foot of Mount Hermon. It was a city dominated by immoral activities and pagan worship. He was there because Jesus didn't want his followers hiding from evil. He wanted them to storm the gates of hell."

Ashlee stated, "OK, I recall reading that. So Jesus was in the northern part of Judea at that time?"

Mathew replied, "Yes, this is also where Jesus asked his disciples in Mark 8:27–29, 'Who do you say that I am?' and Peter replied, 'You are the Son of the living God.' Then in Matthew 16:18, Jesus said, 'You are Peter, and on this rock, I will build my church, and the gates of Hades will not overcome it.' Afterward, they left for home, and it's documented that Jesus went past the Sea of Galilee, so he must have been in the north near Mount Hermon and not Mount Tabor. Jesus, having more alien DNA than any other human, was able to transcend from his physical body to his energy form on his own by using the concentrated energy at that location. So yes, we believe the energy is still there and effective."

"OK then, Mount Hermon's our destination for Ashley and Joe's first mission. James, you go ahead and plan it and let me know what you'll need," Thomas instructed.

"Great! Let's do it." Joe smirked.

CHAPTER TEN

ONE WORLD ORDER

Thomas asked Ashlee and Joe to join him in his office. Once they were there, he said, "I need to tell you both everything we know about One World Order. I don't like the idea of sending you on your first mission without you fully understanding what you're up against."

Joe saw the worried expression on Thomas's face. After turning to Ashlee, who nodded, Joe said, "It's OK Thomas. We understand the high stakes involved, but we are committed to fighting this evil with you and the Group."

Thomas replied, "Thank you both for your service and trust, but let me continue briefing you. This evil started thousands of years ago after God stopped King Nimrod from constructing the Tower of Babel. After the king died, his pregnant widow, Semiramis, was distraught, scared, and angry at God. She also faced losing her kingdom because her subjects would most likely appoint a man as the next king. At this time, Semiramis, in desperation, invoked the help of Satanail (Satan), the angel leader of the rebellion against God.

"Satan, earlier known as Lucifer, had been expelled, and he was kept as a prisoner in the second heaven along with some of his closest followers. He doesn't dwell in any one physical location on Earth, but he is confined to the vicinity of the Earth. In that plane, which is just above the astral plane, he can observe and hear everything on Earth but cannot physically interact with humans. He can communicate with humans in their sleep like in a dream and influence their subconscious if they're open to him. Also, Satan and his lesser demons, the fallen angels, engage in spiritual attacks, including demonic possession, against human beings by the use of supernatural powers in order to harm them.

"Most religions believe that demonic possession is an involuntary affliction, but some ancient scrolls indicate that possession can also be voluntary. When the devil entered Judas Iscariot in John 13:27, this was because Judas had continually agreed to Satan's suggestions to betray Jesus, and Judas had wholly submitted to him.

"Semiramis made a pact and offered her unborn baby to Satan as his vessel on Earth so that he might walk among humans, help her retain her kingdom, and lead them. Satan was able to enter the baby's body because it had not yet received a soul. He could use it as he wished and still access the astral plane when needed. With Satan's guidance and help, she proceeded to deify Nimrod upon his death and declared him reborn after her son's birth. Semiramis and her priests then invented many rituals to worship her as the mother of god and her son as a god. She started the worship of Baal and her son Tammuz, who was in reality Satan, as the leader and representative on Earth."

Ashlee blurted, "Wow! So Satan has reincarnated, has a body, and walks among us?"

Thomas answered, "Yes, but that's not the worst of it. Upon Tammuz's death and thereafter, the death of the subsequent leaders, a new unborn baby would be offered to Satan by one of his followers, and this would be his new vessel and representative on Earth. So thousands of years ago, the mother of all secret societies took root in One World Order, with their primary goal of taking control of Earth to establish one government, language, and leader for all humankind and to challenge the gods upon their return.

"They have infiltrated and influenced all nations, governments, cultures, religions, and political and social organizations worldwide for thousands of years. The way they operate is to position themselves in high-ranking government or military posts so that they can take action or give bad advice to a nation's political and military leaders. They create chaos from within that puts them on a path of self-destruction or at war with other countries.

"All over the world, they infiltrate and hijack peaceful protests and movements, no matter the cause or reason, and turn them into violent, chaotic events. They cause mayhem, create anarchy, and undermine all authority. For instance, Occupy Wall Street (OWS) started as a people's movement against economic inequality, corporate greed, big finance, and the influence of money in politics. It began in Zuccotti Park, which was located in New York City's financial district. It lasted fifty-nine days—from September 17 to November 15, 2011.

"The motives resulted in public distrust in the private sector during the aftermath of the great recession in the United States, such as the 2008 bank bailouts, which utilized congressionally appropriated taxpayer funds to create the Troubled Asset Relief Program (TARP). It purchased toxic assets from failing banks and financial institutions. Also, the US Supreme Court ruling in Citizens United v. FEC in January 2010 allowed corporations to spend unlimited amounts on independent political expenditures without government regulation. This angered the people who viewed the ruling. They felt that it was a way for moneyed interests to corrupt public institutions and legislative bodies, such as the United States Congress.

"These protests as reported in the article 'Occupy Wall Street' on Wikipedia led to the wider Occupy movement in the United States and other Western countries. The Canadian anti-consumerist magazine *Adbusters* initiated the call for a protest. The main issues raised by Occupy Wall Street were social and economic inequality, greed, corruption, and the undue influence of corporations on government— particularly from the financial services sector. To achieve their goals, protesters acted on consensus-based decisions made in general assemblies, which emphasized redress through direct action over the petitioning to authorities.

"The protesters were forced out of Zuccotti Park on November 15, 2011. Protesters then focused on occupying banks, corporate headquarters, board meetings, foreclosed homes, college and university campuses, and social media. *Adbusters* then proposed a peaceful occupation of Wall Street to protest corporate influence on democracy, the lack of legal consequences for those who brought about the global crisis of monetary insolvency, and an increasing disparity in wealth.

"Unfortunately, what started as a peaceful movement was hijacked and taken over by groups controlled by One World Order. Some protesters clashed with police in riot gear outside city hall. Their sole aim was to create violence, anarchy, and defiance of authority. Like the Black Lives Matter movement that began in 2013, participants in the movement initially demonstrated against the deaths of numerous African Americans by police actions or while in police custody. These protests became increasingly violent and chaotic as anarchist groups sponsored by the OWO took them over.

"One World Order will use lies, temptation, bribes, blackmail, force, or assassinations whenever necessary to accomplish their objectives. They want to see humankind destroy itself and weaken so that they can take over and rule the world."

Joe then asked, "Is the current identity of Satan known?"

Thomas replied, "The identity of Satan is a top secret and known only to a few high-ranking members of the One World Order secret society. He's rumored to be a very wealthy and powerful politician. Their secret headquarters' location is somewhere in Europe, known only to a core number of members, and it has state-of-the-art computer and communication equipment.

"Satan's front man and right hand is Charles, a well-dressed, stern-looking, middle-aged man of eastern or mideastern European descent, who's responsible for ensuring that all members receive and carry out the orders from the society. They have thousands of cells all over the world and millions of misled, unwitting accomplice followers. They have become the most powerful secret society on the planet.

"As of now, One World Order has managed to fuel the flames of discontent and greed. They have helped start several armed conflicts in the world, and they have managed to create animosity, distrust, and jealousy among many nations. They have incited rioting in many countries, causing significant damage and destruction of property and lives.

"For the past several years, they have increased their efforts to destroy communities all over the world. They have many governments on the verge of collapse, and the world is on the brink of another world war. The world is sitting on a gunpowder keg, ready to explode! This is what One World Order has been hoping for thousands of years: humankind's destruction so that they can take over and rebuild the world to their liking. I know this is a lot to take in, any second thoughts or questions?"

Joe and Ashlee looked at each other and then at Thomas, and with a smile Joe said, "I understand. We're ready whenever you need us."

★★★

Charles looked out at the room full of people working in front of their desk computers. His expression was grim. "Attention everyone, we have identified the individuals whose energy surge was detected a few days ago: Ashlee Martin and Joe N. Key. Unfortunately, they disappeared from their last known location in Sedona, Arizona, in the United States. We were able to track their energy signature to the Flagstaff airport, and then it disappeared. We have not been able to determine what aircraft they boarded or where they were flown to. Since we haven't been able to detect their energy signature, it means they are in a protected and shielded location. We must assume that they are being helped, most probably by our old nemesis, the Group. They pose a threat to our society and objectives and must be stopped at all costs. Send out the order to all our cells throughout the world to find and terminate them on site."

A chorus of, "Yes, sir!" went through the room before each person turned to work on what his or her commander had relegated them to do—annihilate Ashlee and Joe.

CHAPTER ELEVEN

THE MISSION: MOUNT HERMON

In a company car, Ashlee was on her way to a private at the airport, which was to take her and Joe to Israel. She was reflecting on the briefing that she and Joe had received regarding the mission to Mount Hermon. Her mind was trying to deal with everything that was going on, such as the fact that MIA would be scrambling their energy signature while they were in vehicles, cars, planes, etc., owned by the Group, keeping her and Joe safe from detection and tracking from enemy agents.

But she realized now, it was for real. Once they landed and left the safety of their aircraft, One World Order agents would most likely use the thousands of spies and CCTV cameras that had face recognition software to locate them. So it would be only a matter of time—two hours or less—before they were detected and found. Ashlee felt anxious and slightly scared but had an adrenaline rush all at the same time. She could sense the same in Joe, but more than fear, she sensed that he was concerned—for her. She thought that was sweet and smiled.

Joe looked at Ashlee and said, "We're almost there. We shouldn't let our guard down but watch each other's back."

She nodded. Her face was somber. The flight attendant approached them and said, "We'll be landing shortly at the airport in Haifa. A car will be waiting there for you to drive to your destination."

★★★

Ashley and Joe stepped out of the jet and into a beautiful, sunny day outside. It was early May, and the temperature was pleasant. Suddenly, Mia spoke up. "Welcome to Israel. I will be providing you with constant communication with central headquarters."

"That's right," Mary's voice was heard next. "Mia will be your GPS and navigational aid. She'll project a type of virtual holographic image into your brain that only you both can see, and I will be your link to our entire network."

"Great," Joe answered.

A man in a dark suit greeted them at the bottom of the steps with a firm handshake. He looked from Ashlee to Joe and said, "Hello, I'm David. I will be your contact in Israel should you need anything. Here's your car." He preceded to hand Joe the keys to a recent model Audie A8.

They thanked David, got in the car, and drove away. As Joe drove, lines and angles formed into tangible shapes until he had a map in front of his eyes. "Wow, this is great! I can see the virtual road mapped in front of me. This is better than any Google Maps or car navigation display," Joe praised.

Mia replied, "Yes, it is, and I will be giving you driving directions when needed. For now, just follow the virtual map. Go north on Highway 4 to Acre, then east on 85, north on 90, east on 91, and finally north on Highway 98 to the top of Mount Hermon. This route has the least possible sites for potential attacks, and it should take approximately two hours to reach the destination."

"Thank you, Mia," replied Ashlee.

Mary spoke not long after. "I have the coordinates for your destination on Mount Hermon, and Mia will guide you there. You will be going to an area that used to belong to Syria, but it was captured in the 1967 Six-Day War. On the top is the United Nations buffer zone between Syrian and Israeli-occupied territories; it's the world's highest permanently manned UN position. It is known as Hermon Hotel and is located at 2,814 meters' altitude.

"The southern slopes of Mount Hermon extend to the Israeli-occupied portion of the Golan Heights, where the Mount Hermon ski resort is situated with a top elevation of 2,040 meters (6,690 feet). A peak in this area rises to 2,236 meters (7,336 feet), and it's the highest elevation in Israeli-controlled territory. The Mount Hermon ski lodge is unique; security guards check bags at the entrance, and soldiers man the chairlifts.

"The lodge workers are Druze villagers from nearby Majdal Shams, where residents still pledge loyalty to Bashar al-Assad. Before taking this job, Hermon's CEO was a retired general from the Israel Defense Forces, mainly in the Northern Command. The only route to the Hermon ski lodge is a road filled with hairpin turns, which gains some 5,400 feet in elevation over the course of fifteen miles (twenty-four kilometers) from sea level in Galilee's Hula Valley to the base lodge of the ski area. Stay alert at all times. The drive is intimidating in perfect weather, but when clouds roll in, visibility can drop to near zero, and then it can be terrifying. Unfortunately, that's not the only danger; this is also the stronghold of ancient Baal worshipers and for One World Order."

"Thank you, Mary," they answered, and she responded in kind before it fell silent.

"So Ashlee, since we met, we have been on a fast pace and always training. I realized I don't know much about you. We really haven't had a chance to talk much. Do you have any family or a significant other?" asked Joe, glancing at her before looking back at the road.

She shrugged. "My parents died in an auto accident a few years ago. I'm an only child; no, I have no one else. What about you?" She turned to gaze at him.

Joe kept his eyes straight ahead as he answered. "I also was an only child. I never knew my birth parents. I was adopted as a baby, and all I was ever told was that my father put me up for adoption for my safety and benefit. Also, I don't have anyone else. I always felt something was missing in my life, but now, I feel complete and like I'm where I belong." He gave her a smile, and she returned it.

Ashlee turned to stare out the windshield. "I feel the same way. It seems that everything that's happened in our lives—all that we've done—has been to bring us together at this point in time and place."

"I agree," said Joe.

"You're both righter than you think," said Thomas, startling the two. "I didn't mention it before because I didn't want to add to your burden. But One World Order is planning a worldwide event sometime soon, which can't be good. Our intel and sources tell us that they're planning something big, and knowing how evil they are, it worries me very much. So it's imperative that we get you and Koka to full potential as soon as possible. Hopefully, we can be ready for whatever is coming."

"You are almost there, and so far, our satellite monitoring shows everything is clear all around you. You will be arriving at the ski lodge on Mount Hermon. There should be very few tourists this time of the year. Once you reach the upper parking lot, leave your vehicle there, head to the lodge, and buy lift tickets to the very top. Once you're there, Mia will direct you to the exact spot you're to be at," Mary said.

"OK, Mary. Will do," Joe answered.

Joe parked their car, and the two got out and proceeded to the lift. After they got to the top, Mia instructed, "Turn right and follow the trail heading south. There are two viewing points on this trail. The first one is at 950 meters. Pass it and then continue to the second one, which is at 1.3 kilometers; that's the one you want to be—the 33.30 parallel and the site of the highest energy concentration."

Joe and Ashlee went down the trail. As they got closer to their target point, they could feel the energy around them increasing. They looked at each other and nodded, acknowledging each other's awareness. Finally, they reached the spot they were looking for, and Ashlee said, "It's here. I can feel it." Joe nodded at her.

"Yes, this is it," Mary chimed in as soon as they found a comfortable spot on the ground where they could sit back-to-back. "I will monitor the surroundings and alert you if you're in danger so you can pull out of your trance. If tourists approach, they'll most likely not want to disturb you, so I won't bother you unless I believe you're in danger, OK?"

"Yes, thank you," replied Ashlee

Once they were comfortable and sitting back-to-back, Ashlee and Joe went into a total meditation relaxation, as they have done many times before. They opened a gateway above their heads. With a sudden loud noise and bright light, they passed through it and into the astral plane, where they found themselves in an astral body of pure energy.

"I could never get tired of this. It's amazing," Ashlee murmured in awe.

"I know what you mean," Joe agreed. "It really is incredible."

Koka's presence became prominent to them before they heard his voice. "It is great being here again with you both, but it feels different than before. I can feel the energy building inside of me, my consciousness is clearer, and I'm recovering the missing parts of my memory."

Ashlee agreed, "You're right. The intense concentration of energy in this area must be causing it."

Joe added, "I can sense the presence of other beings in this astral plane, and they also are aware of us. Should we be worried?"

"No, we're OK. They are the millions of beings who have lived before. Upon their death, the cosmic energy that's in all living things comes back to join, mix with, and form part of this collective consciousness in the astral plane. As we navigate this plane, we can tap into it and search for answers or beings. This collective consciousness contains all the past knowledge of all beings who have lived."

"Yes, we're living examples. That's why we believe, now more than ever, in the cosmic life force that shrouds us," Ashlee replied on both of their behalves.

Suddenly, Koka exclaimed, "Wait a minute! My memory has partially recovered, and I now know what we have to do. Also, as I connected to the cosmic energy, I could sense the urgency of what was happening on Earth. Because our conscious minds are connected, we're able to share our knowledge, so now you know what I know and what has to be done. We have to be careful.; powerful forces want to stop us. Even here, I can sense the presence of a powerful evil being."

Ashlee and Joe pulled on the silver cord and returned to their bodies. Ashlee asked, "Mary, are you there?"

"Yes, I'm here. How did it go?"

"We'll tell you about it on our way back, but we must leave now.

Mia, find us a safe route back to the Haifa airport and monitor the surrounding area with the satellite because we are going to have company—the bad type," Ashlee informed them urgently.

Mia replied, "Yes, it will only take a few seconds. Done; I have it. You will be going back through the Israeli town of Neve Ativ, which is also home to the families who own Hermon Ski Lodge, a privately operated corporation. I will be guiding you. Go back down Highway 98. Once you pass lower parking lot 3, a road junction will be on the right side; take it. It's a country road. Stay on your left at the Y-split, and it will take you to Neve Ativ. More importantly, you will avoid the town of Majdal Shams and the suspicious black SUV that's rapidly approaching from the south."

They got into the car and sped away. Right as they got on the highway, Ashlee said, "There's a black SUV following us. It must be the one that Mary warned us about. See if you can lose it."

Joe looked into the rearview mirror and spotted the vehicle. He noticed that it was gaining on them quickly. Joe smiled and replied, "Hold on. Now you're going to see my driving skills." And with this, he sped up and raced down the narrow road. He made some harrowing sharp turns close to the edge until he could no longer see the SUV in his rearview mirror. Joe then took the country road to Neve Ativ. Then he asked, "Mary, we managed to lose the SUV that was following us. Were you able to make out any details?"

"I'm on it. I have them on our satellite view. The infrared camera detects four individuals. I'll keep an eye on them and inform you of any changes," Mary responded.

"Thanks, Mary," Ashlee replied.

Ashlee and Joe reached the town of Neve Ativ and continued south on Route 989 until they got to Highway 99 near Sa'ar Falls and by the Druze market.

Mia said, "Now head west until you see the exit for the Banias Spring Church. Then take it."

Ashley was surprised with the instructions and asked, "I thought you were directing us back to the airport?"

Mia replied, "Mary just gave me an updated satellite video showing the black SUV that was back on Mount Hermon. It turned around, and it has been on your rear and not far behind you. Also, there's a second SUV coming fast on Highway 99 toward your location."

"Great! So what's the plan?" asked Joe.

Mary answered, "A helicopter being piloted by one of our agents is on its way to pick you up and take you to the airport. You need to hurry and get to the parking lot on the north side of the Byzantine Church, which is just north of the ancient ruins at Caesarea Philippi. Its ETA is ten minutes."

Ashlee and Joe looked at each other and nodded. They knew that their fighting skills would be tested. They took the exit to Banias Spring Church. It wasn't a great road, but they had to continue to their destination, which was just a few minutes away. Suddenly, there was a loud metallic, grinding noise, and they felt a strong push forward. Ashley turned and saw the SUV right behind them, pushing and crashing into their rear. Joe tried to outrun it, but he couldn't. As they reached Banias Church, a sudden crash and push from behind sent their car off the road and into a ditch.

Joe looked at Ashlee and said, "We're very close to our landing zone. We can make it. Let's just take care of our company first. What do you say?"

Ashley grinned mischievously at him before gazing toward the SUV, where four men were walking toward them. "I'll take the two on the left and bolt out of the car."

Joe killed the engine and unlocked the doors with a loud exhale. "I guess the other two are for me." He pushed the door open and also rushed out.

The men from the SUV were dressed in black tactical gear and wearing masks. As they approached Ashlee and Joe, they raised their automatic weapons, but before they could use them, Ashlee and Joe raised their hands with the bracelets, giving Mia a mental order to use stun mode. The bracelets fired an energy beam, and the men dropped the heated weapons and stumbled briefly in a daze.

The men recovered and ran toward Ashlee and Joe. They attacked, using flying kicks that were synchronized with fist and arm blows.

They were martial arts' experts by the fighting skills they exhibited. But you could see their surprised faces when they realized that Ashlee and Joe were formidable foes, who were counterattacking all their moves.

Ashlee fought with two of them simultaneously. She went back and forth with fist blows, leg kicks, and flying through the air. It was as if she could anticipate their movements just enough to avoid being hit and to be able to land blows to their faces and bodies. Eventually, she was able to dominate them, rendering them unconscious. Ashlee could sense Joe was having the same experience fighting the other two men from the SUV. She knew that he could anticipate their movements and avoid being hit while landing blows at will, which he did. It seemed like a well-choreographed fight, but with real blows. Eventually, he also rendered them unconscious. During the whole time they were engaged in fighting, they were aware of each other's location, as if they were seeing it from a spectator's point of view.

Joe turned to and asked Ashley, "Did you have that same feeling?"

Ashlee nodded. "Yes, I believe that was Koka helping out by keeping us aware of our location regarding each other."

"Good." Joe grabbed her hand and tugged on it. "Now let's run to the extraction zone. It's just up the road and nearby."

"Let's go," answered Ashlee as they started running.

★★★

They were almost to the parking lot when they found themselves under automatic gunfire. As they ran, dodging the bullets, Joe turned and saw that the second SUV had caught up with them. There were also four men in black gear firing at them. Joe yelled at Ashlee to keep running and then stopped, turned, and cupped his hand, creating an energy plasma ball, which he launched at them with a loud noise and blinding light. After a few seconds, Joe and Ashlee turned. All four men were on the ground, moaning but alive.

"Wow," Ashlee said, panting, "I didn't realize you were that good at producing plasma balls."

"Me either," he heaved out. They both shared a look before breaking out into laughter. Then they continued on their way.

Right then, the helicopter landed. The pilot smiled and asked, "Do you want a lift?"

Ashlee and Joe laughed. "You bet," Joe said, smiling.

Once on board the jet, Thomas came online and said, "Welcome. It's good to have you on board sound and safe. I understand you had a rather exciting finale. Mia informed us you handled it very efficiently."

"Thank you, sir," replied Joe.

"Was the mission successful?" Thomas inquired.

"Very much so," replied Ashlee. "We're going to share all the information we found out and tell you everything, but first, you have to direct this flight to our new destination."

"And where is that?" asked Thomas.

"We're going to the cave east of Göbekli Tepe in Turkey."

CHAPTER TWELVE

GÖBEKLI TEPE

Thomas said, "OK, the pilot has instructions to fly you to Paphos International Airport in Cyprus; we have friends there who will help. After you land, an agent of ours will take you to a converted helicopter research vessel, which will be waiting for you. It will take you to a point offshore but near the Turkey-Syrian border. The ship will wait for nightfall, and then a special stealth helicopter will take you to the cave east of Göbekli Tepe. James is working on all the logistics for your mission, so that is being taken care of. Could you tell us what's going on?"

Ashlee replied, "While we were in the astral plane, Koka was able to partially recover his memory. As he connected to the cosmic energy, he could sense the urgency of what was happening on Earth. Since our conscious minds are connected, we're able to share our knowledge; now we know what he knows and what has to be done. We have to be careful because powerful forces want to stop us, and even there, we could sense the presence of a powerful evil being. It seems that a worldwide event is being planned by One World Order and its proxies. They believe the gods are returning soon and want to prepare for a confrontation against them. They need to have control of the earth's armies and nuclear weapons so they can use them. To this end, they are pushing to bring the world under their control as soon as possible. They will first eliminate the governments or countries that are opposing them or at least weaken them so they can easily be taken over. This is being planned for some time soon."

Thomas and the rest of the team at headquarters were silent for a moment, and then suddenly, they all exclaimed things like, "Wow!" "The gods are returning," and "A possible war among us here on Earth and then against them."

Thomas stated, "We knew they were up to something, but this is really incredible and scary."

Joe then said, "There's more; Koka also remembered portions of his life before he died, including the last place he was at: the cave east of Göbekli Tepe."

Ashlee added, "He believes there's energy trapped in that cave, which was left by his body, would help strengthen him, and help his memory recover faster."

Thomas replied, "Well, we need him to recover as soon as possible, and maybe he can help us deal with what's coming. In the meantime, you two should rest. It will be a short flight to Cyprus."

Ashlee and Joe reclined their seats and closed their eyes for some well-deserved relaxation meditation. A short time later, a flight attendant said softly, "We have arrived at Paphos International Airport."

Joe and Ashlee opened their eyes, straightened their seats, and said, "Thank you."

After the plane landed and the door was opened, Ashlee and Joe stepped out and took a deep breath. It was a beautiful evening with a wonderful breeze and fresh air. Mary came online and said, "An agent of ours named Nicholas is waiting to take you to Paphos's harbor and a waiting ship. It will be a twenty-five-minute drive via B6. Mia will monitor the area to make sure you're not being followed."

Mia replied, "Yes, I will monitor and make sure your surroundings are safe. Also, I have downloaded the route to the harbor into the car so your driver can follow it. I'm scrambling your signals so no one can detect you while you're in transit to the ship."

They saw a man waving at them, so they walked toward him. He said, "Welcome to Cyprus. I'm Nicholas, and I'm to take you to our group's ship that's waiting in the harbor."

Joe answered, "Hi, Nicholas. Thank you. It is nice being here. Let's go."

Soon after they arrived at the harbor, a small boat appeared with two sailors in white uniforms, who were waiting for them. One of them said, "Hi! I'm Robert. We are to take you to our research ship, which is anchored in the harbor. Please get in." Ashlee and Joe thanked them and got into the boat, which then made its way out to the ship. It was only a fifteen-minute ride.

Soon, they found themselves on the staircase that went up to the deck area. When they reached it, a familiar voice said, "Hi, you two. It's about time you got here."

Ashlee and Joe looked up. Then Ashlee exclaimed, "Simon! Nice to see you, but how did you get here?"

Simon replied, "It's also nice to see you both. Well, you see, the moment you were sent on your assignment to Mount Hermon, I came here as a backup for you. I needed to be nearby just in case you ran into problems. Because I'm a martial arts' expert and military tactician, I had to be close by to assess the situation and design a new plan of action if needed. As you see, you were never alone; we're all in it together."

Ashlee smiled and then said, "Well, I for one am happy to see you and know that you've got our backs."

Joe chuckled, nodded, and then asked, "So why the ship? Why not fly into an airport near our target and then drive there as we did before at Mount Hermon?"

Simon answered, "Well, it's not that easy; Göbekli Tepe, due to its proximity to the Syrian border, is a war-sensitive zone. Turkey's government is not going to allow us anywhere near that area, no matter the reason. So we have a plan to get you there after dark using our stealth helicopter. It now has a cloaking feature, which we developed from ancient technological instructions. We'll be able to fly low, reach our target point, and get back before they even know we were ever there. We'll leave at midnight; by then, we'll be close enough to the coast."

Ashlee and Joe nodded. Then Joe said, "Great! Let's do it."

It was nearly midnight, and Ashlee and Joe were in the helicopter with James and two other crew members. Then Thomas came on the line. "Hi! Are you ready for this mission?"

"Yes," they all answered.

"Great! Mary, with the help of Mia, is monitoring the surroundings, including airspace, to make sure you don't run into any problems."

"That's correct," said Mary. "Mia and I will keep you informed of any changes. As of now, you are good to go."

And with that, the helicopter took off. Very quietly, it was on its way to the coordinates that would take it to the target site east of Göbekli Tepe, a cave on a hillside just south of the town of Ortaoren. It was a short flight, and soon, they reached their target.

They exited the helicopter and worked their way to the site. It had been years since the Group's last mission to the cave, but although it took a while, they followed Thomas's instructions, and they were able to find the entrance to the cave once again. Once they identified it, the two crew members started using a pick and shovel to expose and reopen the entrance. After a couple of hours, they finally broke through, and Ashley, Joe, and Simon entered.

Ashlee exclaimed, "Wow! This is amazing." Both Joe and Simon nodded.

Simon then said, "From the photos I reviewed back at headquarters, everything seems to be the same."

They saw murals with paintings and glyphs that depicted scenes of humans performing chores, such as planting, taking measurements of the sky, building structures, etc. All of this was done while being observed or supervised by beings who were at least two to three times taller than the humans were. They had beards, wore robes, had tall cone-shaped hats, and had wings. Also, in the middle of the chamber, there was a stone slab approximately sixteen feet long, five feet wide, and two feet thick resting on stone pedestals, which were four feet high, five feet wide, and two feet thick at each end.

Ashley turned to look at Joe, who nodded. Then she said to Simon, "It's time for us to enter the astral plane; Koka is calling us."

"OK, he replied, I'll stand guard at the entrance."

They sat down back-to-back. Just as they had done many times before, they entered a state of meditation. Soon, there was a loud sound and a flash of light, and they found themselves in the astral plane. Koka then said, "Nice to see you again. I can feel my energy building up rapidly."

"Great!" Ashlee said.

Joe then asked, "Is this place familiar to you?"

Koka answered, "Yes, it is. This is the final resting place of my physical body. It lay on that stone slab for thousands of years until it turned completely into dust. The residual energy freed from my body was trapped in here. But now I have assimilated it, and it's allowed me to recover more of my memory and increase my strength."

"That's great!" Ashlee replied.

Joe asked, "What else can you remember?"

Koka replied, "Thousands of years ago, I was helping humans build boats and underground shelters in preparation for a cataclysm that was to come. I found myself trying to help groups of humans all over the world. You know them by the names your archeologists have given them: Paleo-Indians in North America, Central America, and South America. The Ubaidians were prehistoric people who lived in the region of Mesopotamia before the Sumerians and many others throughout the world did. A flood was unleashed on the world to eliminate humans, but with the preparations we had done, many survived. Afterward, I guided them to underground shelters, where they remained for hundreds of years. During this time, the earth went back to Ice Age temperatures and glaciers, which lasted a thousand years. After it was safe to emerge and live on the surface again, I helped them drain the marshes for agriculture, develop trade, and establish industries, including weaving, leatherwork, metalwork, masonry, and pottery."

Ashley said, "That's incredible. So what happened to you?"

"Koka replied, "Although I had a long lifespan of several thousand years. I was not immortal, but my DNA was. I could pass it to offspring. When enough of it found its way back and came into contact with itself again, it had the ability to recombine itself and recreate me partially or completely. My time on Earth was coming to an end, and many of the humans that I had helped wanted to help preserve me, so they provided young women whom I could pass some of my DNA to. I left instructions in many storage sites regarding how to bring me back and build weapons and tracking devices and the covenant made with the Creator, which all of us have to follow and for which he will judge us on his return. I died, and the local humans put me in here, which I had prepared beforehand."

Ashlee was in awe. Joe asked, "So what now? Where do we go from here?"

Koka answered, "I remember before returning to this place that I was in South America helping the local humans there. We were storing information in a cave, which was written down on metal sheets and stone tablets. Afterward, it would help them to rebuild and survive in case I was not around. We should go there and retrieve them so we can find a way to stop One World Order and figure out when the Creator is returning."

Ashlee then said, "I think we all know where we have to go. Also, does anyone besides me have this uneasy feeling?"

Koka replied, "That is the same evil entity I sensed before. It's getting stronger, and I believe it's trying to track us." They all exclaimed agreed that it was time to go while pulling on the silver cords.

Ashlee and Joe exited the cave, and upon seeing them, Simon, who had been standing guard, asked, "Is everything OK?"

"Yes," Ashlee replied. "Let's seal the cave entrance so we can leave as soon as possible."

After they had finished, they got in their helicopter and started back to the ship. About halfway there, Mia came online saying, "You have an unidentified jet heading toward you. At this time, it's not possible to determine its origin or intentions, but it's headed your way."

"Thank you, Mia," Simon replied as they started to make defensive preparations. Simon then said, "I don't know how they are tracking us while we have the cloaking device turned on, but it's imperative that you two survive. If it comes to the point where we are in danger of being shot down, I need you to enter this room in the back. It will be automatically released. It's a self-contained capsule capable of withstanding an explosion, is waterproof, floats, and has self-inflating balloons that will break any fall. It has a tracking device, so the group will find you no matter where you are."

Ashlee and Joe entered the escape pod. A few seconds later, the helicopter started making evasive maneuvers and releasing countermeasures—flares and chaffs to deflect missiles. Ashlee heard an explosion nearby and felt an intense shaking and vibration. She looked at Joe, who smiled and nodded, making her feel reassured. The flares were decoys that confused heat-seeking missiles by creating an alternative target. It seemed to be working so far. Suddenly, they heard a loud explosion, and then everything went silent.

The escape pod door opened, and Simon, smiling, said, "OK, you can come out now."

"What happened? Is it all over?" they asked. "Are we safe?"

Simon answered, "Yes, thank God it's over. Apparently, that jet left itself exposed every time it fired a missile, and someone on the ground used a surface-to-air missile and shot it down."

Mia came online and added, "No government or military has claimed that aircraft, which leads me to believe it was a One World Order jet. I do not detect any other dangers; you should be arriving at the ship in ten minutes."

Once on board the ship, it was a short trip back to the Paphos harbor. There, Nicholas was waiting for them and took Ashlee and Joe back to the airport, where they boarded their private jet. Simon stayed behind; he was to take a commercial flight back to New York. Thomas then welcomed them back on board and informed them of how happy and relieved the whole team was that they had survived their ordeal with the enemy jet. Then he asked, "Was this mission successful, and where to now?"

Ashlee replied, "Yes, it was, and we'll tell you all about it, but first, we need to set a flight path to Ecuador."

CHAPTER THIRTEEN

ECUADOR

Thomas said, "I have informed the pilot to fly you to Ecuador. Give him the exact location you're going to, and we'll also have some of our agents waiting there to assist in your mission."

"Great, we're going to Cuenca, Ecuador," Ashlee replied

"OK. What for?" asked Thomas.

Ashlee leaned back in her seat before she began speaking. "Remember, Thomas, when you told us about how the indigenous people gave Father Crespi gifts of ancient artifacts to thank him for his work and for helping them? They said that the items brought to him had been found in subterranean tunnels and caves in the jungles of Ecuador, which spanned more than two hundred kilometers, starting from the village of Cuenca. The indigenous people considered them sacred, so the tunnel locations were never revealed, not even to Father Crespi. They are still unknown. Also, many were killed by the indigenous people when they searched for the mysterious subterranean tunnels with the hidden treasure."

Thomas replied, "Yes, that's what I had said."

Ashlee continued, "Well, we are going back to search for some ancient relics that should be very helpful in restoring Koka and in fighting One World Order."

Luke, the historian, then exclaimed, "But there are no records of any ancient relics found down there other than the ones we have."

Then John said, "Also, there have been archeological expeditions to search the caves down there in Ecuador without results. The rumor of the ancient relics being stored in the Cueva de los Tayos was false."

Thomas said, "What we know for sure is that in 1969, Juan Móricz, who claimed to have explored and discovered mounds of gold, unusual sculptures, and a metallic library, undertook an expedition to Cueva de los Tayos. He said that these items were in artificial tunnels that had been created by a lost civilization with help from extraterrestrial beings. As a result of his claims, an expedition to Cueva de los Tayos was organized by Stan Hall of Scotland in 1976. It was one of the largest cave explorations ever undertaken. It involved over a hundred people, including experts in a variety of fields, British and Ecuadorian military personnel, a film crew, and former American astronaut Neil Armstrong."

"Wow!" exclaimed Ashlee. "I didn't realize such an expedition had taken place."

Thomas said, "Oh, yes, the team also included eight experienced British cavers, who thoroughly explored the cave and conducted an accurate survey to produce a detailed map of it. It was a complete bust; they didn't find anything regarding what Móricz had claimed. The lead researcher met with Móricz's indigenous source, who claimed that they had investigated the wrong cave and that the real cave was secret."

Joe sighed and said, "Well, they were searching in the wrong place. Moricz's indigenous source, whom they met with, told the truth: They had investigated the wrong cave. Remember what the indigenous people told Father Crespi: The tunnels and caves spanned more than two hundred kilometers, starting from the village of Cuenca. Cueva de los Tayos is over two hundred kilometers east of Cuenca and takes over three hours to get to by car, which is not near the town at all."

In unison, the whole team asked, "Where then?"

Ashlee said, "Well, while we were in the astral plane, Koka remembered that he had been helping the native population prepare for the cataclysm that was going to happen. He helped them enlarge caves and tunnels so they could store animals and food. It would hold thousands of people. Koka remembered preparing special locations in these facilities throughout the world to store information on metal and

98

stone plates. These would have the knowledge necessary for humans to rebuild and survive once they could go back to the surface. Also, they contained the instructions and warnings from the Creator, which they were to follow in order to stay in harmony with him and the earth. Among these locations is the one in Cuenca. It's just on the outskirts east of town at the Mirador Paccha. Mia, I'm sending you the address: 433F+26H, Cuenca-Azogues, Cuenca, Ecuador."

Mia answered, "Got it; I'm already plotting the route."

Joe then said, "There's an entrance to a cave covered with bushes approximately thirty feet below the southeast ledge of this point at these coordinates: 2°53'52.9"S 78°55'36.1"W. Koka believes it still may contain what we're looking for."

Luke said, "Wow! That's incredible. I never would have believed a historical treasure like that was that close to Cuenca all this time." Everyone agreed.

Thomas was the next to add, "OK, you two rest, and I'll have James put together a plan for your mission. Do you have any questions?"

Joe first looked at Ashley, who nodded, and then replied, "Nope, we're good." Then they proceeded to recline their seats completely and fell asleep almost immediately while looking at each other.

Several hours later, Ashlee and Joe were awakened by a very soft melody. "Good morning," Mia said.

"Good morning," they both replied.

The flight attendant walked in and said, "We are a couple of hours from our destination: Aeropuerto Mariscal Lamar in Cuenca, Ecuador. In the meantime, I'll bring you breakfast and a change of clothes. There's a bathroom and shower in the back of the plane for your convenience."

Ashlee replied, "Thank you very much; I need that."

"Me too," said Joe with a smile.

After they had eaten and freshened up while talking about the day ahead, they were interrupted by a beep from their imbedded chip. It was Thomas, who said, "James has your next mission all planned out for you, so I'm going to let him go over it with you."

"Great!" They answered.

Joe and Ashlee squinted as their communication chips made a screeching sound. Then James said, "Hi, Ashlee and Joe. You will be arriving at the Cuenca airport, where Thomas has arranged for our contacts in Ecuador to get a special clearance for both of you to enter the country. You will be met by one of our agents, who will assist you and drive you to Mirador Paccha. Mia will be directing the navigational part. She will lead you to the location of the hidden cave. Our agent has the equipment you'll need to repel down to the cave and back up. Afterward, he'll drive you back to the airport and then home. Any questions?"

Joe replied, "No, it's pretty clear what we have to do."

"Yes," Ashlee agreed.

The pilot announced over the intercom, "Please prepare for landing. We have arrived at Cuenca, Ecuador. It's a beautiful day—sixty-two degrees Fahrenheit and sunny and clear. It's 6:00 a.m. local time."

Ashlee stated, "It's kind of weird that we're at the equator, and yet it's a cool morning."

Mia automatically replied, "Cuenca is located in the south-central inter-Andean region of Ecuador—the Paute river basin—at an altitude of 2,538 meters above sea level and with a temperate Andean climate averaging 16.3 °Celsius all year around. It has two distinct seasons: a rainy season, which peaks in January and February, and a dry season, which peaks in July and August. Would you like a brief summary of its history?"

Everyone laughed, and then Ashlee answered, "Sure, Mia, why not?"

Mia started narrating that it had been locally called Cuenca of the Andes or Athens of Ecuador for its architecture, cultural diversity, and contribution. It was founded on April 12, 1557, on the ruins of the Incan city of Tomebamba, by Gil Ramírez Dávalos, under the orders of the viceroy of Peru, Andrés Hurtado de Mendoza.

"During the twentieth century, the city continued to grow, promoting education and culture. In 1999, its historic center was declared a UNESCO World Heritage Site. It is one of Ecuador's most important administrative, economic, financial, and commercial centers. Cuenca has also established itself as an international tourist attraction. The Cañari, then the Inca, and then the Spanish occupied the region in the last two millennia, each renaming it in its own language. Now the capital city is called Cuenca and the province Azuay."

Joe then said, "Thank you, Mia. That's very informative." Both Ashlee and Joe chuckled.

Mia replied, "You are welcome."

The jet landed, and after the flight attendant opened the door, she turned to Ashlee and Joe, saying, "Welcome to Cuenca, Ecuador. You may disembark anytime you wish." They replied with polite thank-yous and proceeded to exit the plane. Once outside, they paused to take in a deep breath of the beautiful, cool morning air.

Joe exclaimed, "That feels good," and Ashlee agreed with a smile.

Thomas, their contact, then cautioned them. "Be careful, you two. Remember, the One World Order agents are searching for you."

They replied, "Roger that."

Mary added, "Mia has the route mapped out for you. She'll be guiding you to your target point."

Grateful, they responded, "Thanks."

James, another member of their team, provided further instructions, saying, "You are meeting with Felipe, our agent. He'll be waiting for you in a black Humvee. He'll drive you to your destination and help set up the equipment. If you need anything else, just ask him. Afterward, he'll bring you back to the airport. Do you have any questions?" Ashlee and Joe exchanged a glance and then told him they didn't. Ashlee and Joe scanned their surroundings and spotted Felipe waving at them next to the black Humvee.

He introduced himself as they walked toward him. "Ashlee and Joe, welcome to Cuenca. I'm Felipe, your guide." They greeted him warmly and said that they wanted to get started.

Mia chimed in with directions, "I have programmed your navigational system to take you to the top of Mirador Paccha. First, you'll head southwest toward Avenue España to Avenue of the

Américas and then take the Azogues-Cuenca Pan-American Road to
Vía Paccha. Continue driving on Via Paccha and then take the Mirador
Paccha exit. From there, it's a few minutes' drive to Mirador Paccha."
Joe and Ashlee expressed their gratitude by thanking Mia.

As they drove through the city, they couldn't help but appreciate
the beauty of its architecture, the majestic mountains surrounding it,
and the clear blue sky above. The early hour meant that there was only
a little traffic, making their journey a pleasant one. Felipe explained
to Ashlee and Joe that Mirador Paccha was a popular view for both
locals and tourists, offering a breathtaking view of the city in the valley
below. He also mentioned that he and the other members of their
group were unaware of any caves in the area they were headed to.
Without revealing too much, Joe informed him that a reliable source
had given them this lead.

Finally, they arrived at the top of the mountain and Mirador
Paccha. They parked their vehicle, and Joe asked as he walked, "Now
what, Mia?"

Mia promptly replied, "Continue walking southeast approximately
fifty feet. Then head toward the edge." Joe followed her instructions
until Mia exclaimed, "Stop! You're right above the coordinates you
gave me."

Joe said, "Thank you, Mia," and then asked Ashlee, "Did you get
that?"

She replied, "Ten four. I'm on my way with the equipment."

Joe said, "Roger that."

Ashlee and Felipe joined Joe at the spot on the edge of the cliff
where Mia had directed him to. They proceeded to anchor two metallic
rope holders firmly into the ground. Once they were secure, they
threw the ropes they were going to rappel down with over the edge.
It was evident that the ropes extended approximately seventy-five feet
down. Joe turned to Ashley and asked, "Are you ready?"

She replied, "Let's do it."

He nodded and then turned to Felipe, saying, "You wait for us here
and watch our six, OK?"

Felipe replied, "Yes, sir."

Joe and Ashlee grabbed their ropes and began their descent of the face of the cliff. The face was covered with bushes and small trees. They had descended about thirty to forty feet when Ashlee suddenly exclaimed, "Wait, what's that?" She pointed to a dark depression behind some bushes.

Joe replied, "Let's find out." He started clearing away the bushes, and as he did, he revealed what lay beneath. He gasped. "Oh, my God, do you see this, Ashlee?"

She replied, "I sure do. Koka was right; it's an entrance to a cave." They cautiously entered the cave and found themselves in a wide chamber. It was pitch dark, and they couldn't see much, so Ashlee retrieved some flashlights from their backpacks. With their flashlights in hand, Joe and Ashlee ventured deeper into the cave, discovering a network of tunnels. They covered around three hundred meters and encountered several expansive caverns connected by tunnels, which seemed to stretch on endlessly. Among the artifacts they came across were bones and fragments of pottery, but there were no signs of any metal or stone relics.

Joe told Ashlee that he had tried contacting Mia and the rest of the team but had had no success, most likely due to the thick layers of earth and minerals surrounding them. Joe turned to Ashlee and asked, "Are you thinking the same thing that I am?"

She nodded and replied, "Yes, let's try Koka." They sat down on the ground back-to-back and entered into a deep meditation, as they had done many times before.

As they opened a gateway above their heads, a sudden burst of light and noise transported them into the astral plane, where they existed as pure energy. In the astral plane, Koka's voice resonated. "Being here has allowed me to recover more fragments of my memory. I recall being in these tunnels long ago. I assisted the people who lived here, helped them get organized, and delegated responsibilities, such as managing water and controlling plagues. Their technology was advanced, making it easy for me to guide them on how to survive the cataclysm underground. They understood that they needed to remain underground for many generations and until it was safe to return to the surface. I left them written records on sheets of metal and stone, which were designed to withstand the test of time, along with instructions for their survival once they resurfaced. I also left the covenant they made with the Creator."

Joe contemplated the situation and said, "Well, it appears that everything is gone. Do you have any ideas?"

Koka replied, "Yes, I have successfully made contact with the entities who were trying to reach me. However, I also sense the presence of an evil being here, who is searching for us. We must leave immediately." With that, they tugged on their silver cords, and Ashlee and Joe instantly were back in their physical bodies.

Ashlee said, "Let's work our way back to the entrance."

Joe replied, "Roger that."

They retraced their steps and reached the entrance, only to find that the ropes were no longer hanging outside. Ashlee asked, "Mia, can you hear me?"

Mia's voice came through. "Yes, Ashlee. As you ventured deeper into the cave, I lost contact with you both, but our communication is now restored."

"Good," said Ashlee. "We have a problem; our rappel ropes are missing from the opening. Can you see Felipe?"

Mia replied, "Yes, our satellite image shows he's lying motionless on the ground, and four other people are just above your location, waiting."

Joe then interjected, "Mary, what are our options?"

Mary responded, "We're working on it. There appears to be an extensive network of caves and tunnels stretching for a hundred miles or more."

Suddenly, Ashlee grabbed Joe's arm and asked, "Do you feel it too?"

Joe nodded and replied, "Yes. Mia, could you use satellite imaging and ground-penetrating radar to create a map of the caverns and tunnels?"

Mia said, "Yes, Joe, I can."

Joe replied, "Great. Let's do it."

Mary addressed them. "Joe, we're all here wondering what your plan is."

Ashlee explained. "Koka will guide us from the astral plane. We'll use the tunnels to reach the center of Cuenca aided by the map Mia is preparing. He knows the way to the old cathedral catacombs at the corner of C. Luis Cordero and Mariscal Sucre."

Mary said, "That's wonderful. We'll have another agent waiting for you there to take you to the airport. Let us know what else you need, and from all of us, good luck and be careful." Joe and Ashlee expressed their gratitude by saying thanks.

Ashlee and Joe exchanged knowing glances, understanding each other's unspoken thoughts. They nodded in silent agreement and began walking deeper into the underground labyrinth. Mia had downloaded a map of the underground caves and tunnels into their minds using satellite imaging and penetrating radar data. They relied on it as a guide. They were synchronized with subtle nudges of energy from Koka, which directed them to go straight, turn right, or left. Hours passed as they traversed caverns of various sizes, interconnected by tunnels, which occasionally led to the surface. Finally, Ashlee said, "We're here. There's a small room on the other side of this wall, which leads to the catacombs."

Joe replied, "All right, let's find something to break the wall."

Ashlee countered, "Joe, we are the something that can break the wall," and she smiled.

Joe chuckled. "Oh, yes, I keep forgetting the skills we've developed."

Ashlee and Joe focused their energy on forming plasma balls. With a nod to each other, they launched them simultaneously. A thunderous noise and blinding light filled the chamber as the wall shook and buckled, but it didn't entirely collapse. "Wow!" they exclaimed.

Ashlee suggested, "Let's do it again." Concentrating, they created larger plasma balls and on a coordinated signal, released them with tremendous force, generating intense energy, noise, and blinding light. This time, the wall crumbled and fell, creating a wide opening into a brick-lined chamber with a hallway leading to a stairway.

"Yes!" they shouted, amazed. They laughed and hugged each other.

Suddenly, Mia's voice came through. "Joe, Ashlee, you have four visitors waiting on the corner just outside the catacomb building. I believe they are the enemy agents who were tracking you."

Mary quickly added, "Help is on the way. It'll take our agents fifteen to twenty minutes to get there, so hold on and lie low until they do."

Ashlee and Joe exchanged glances; their smiles told a silent story of determination. They began walking toward the hallway and ascended the masonry stairway, which led to a room with an opening in the ceiling and a stone staircase that reached the top. Upon emerging, they found themselves in a spacious chamber with an exit leading to the outside. As they stepped out of the building, the four individuals that Mia had warned them about came into view. Joe turned to Ashlee and asked, "Are you ready?"

Ashlee responded with confidence, "You bet," and a smile graced her lips.

Joe quickly formulated a plan, "You take the two on the left, and I'll handle the other two. Ready? Go!"

Ashlee confronted the two assailants on the left. With the help of her ability to read and project thoughts and by using her martial arts skills, she delivered precise strikes with her fists, arms, and legs. After a few minutes of exchanging blows, she gradually started to overcome her opponents, defeating and disabling them with relative ease. She then rushed to assist Joe, who was engaged in a tougher battle with his opponents. With Ashlee's support, Joe gained the upper hand and managed to overcome his adversaries. He chuckled and admitted, "Well, if I could anticipate their moves like you do, I could counteract them more efficiently, but I work with what I have." They shared a laugh.

Mary's voice broke in at that moment, "The black Humvee that just arrived contains our agents. They'll escort you to the airport, and it won't take more than a few minutes." Grateful, Ashlee and Joe thanked Mary.

Back on board the plane, they inquired about Felipe's condition. Thomas reassured them. "He's going to be all right. He sustained a concussion but is otherwise OK. He's under overnight observation at the hospital and should be discharged in the morning."

Ashlee responded, "Great!" James then asked about the mission's outcome. Ashlee explained, "It appears that the ancient artifacts were likely removed by One World Order. We found no traces of them in any of the tunnels and caverns we explored."

Luke chimed in, "I'm not surprised. The OWO has been flooding the area with fake relics and claiming they belonged to Father Crespi in an attempt to discredit his findings and convince the world it was all a hoax. They'll stop at nothing to hide the truth."

When Thomas inquired about their next steps, Joe said, "The mission didn't fail entirely. While we were there, we initiated a session to access the astral plane. We sought Koka's help in locating the ancient relics since we didn't find any in the cave. Koka managed to make contact with the astral energy of beings who had been trying to reach him for some time. With their help, Koka recovered enough memory and energy to connect with them. Now we know where to continue our search."

Thomas responded, "That's great news. So where are we heading next, and what are we looking for?"

Ashlee answered, "We'll fill you in, but first, instruct the pilot to chart a course for China."

Thomas agreed, "OK, you'll brief us on the way."

CHAPTER FOURTEEN

IN THE BEGINNING

"I already informed the pilot to fly you to China. Just give him the location so we can also arrange for an agent to meet you there and assist in your mission," Thomas said.

"Great, we're going to the Banpo Museum in Xi'an, Shaanxi," Ashlee replied.

"OK. What for?" asked Thomas.

Ashlee leaned back in her seat to get comfortable before she began speaking. "As you already know, Koka, Joe, and I share our thoughts and knowledge during our astral body experience. What I'm about to tell you is thanks to Koka, who was able to contact some entities who had been searching for him. In 1937, an archeological expedition in the Bayan Har Mountains led by Chi Pu Tei found 716 granite discs with tiny hieroglyph-like markings dating back twelve thousand years ago. Star maps and mummies with thin bodies and unusually enormous heads were also at the site. After more than two decades of work at the Academy of Prehistory in Beijing, Chinese archeologists and linguists managed to translate the markings."

"They concluded that extraterrestrials had carved the discs in the aftermath of their crash in the Sino-Tibetan border region. These conclusions were published by Tsum Um Nui in an academic journal, but they were met with ridicule. Tsum then left for Japan in self-imposed exile and died shortly after that. The discs measured up to thirty centimeters in diameter and carried two grooves in the form of a double spiral, which originated from a hole in the center. Hieroglyphs were inscribed within the grooves and visible with a magnifying glass.

"In 1966, the story was republished by Vyacheslav Zaitsev in the Soviet magazine *Sputnik*. Zaitsev added that several discs had been shipped to Moscow at the request of Soviet researchers, who discovered that they contained large amounts of cobalt and other metals, behaved as electrical conductors, and produced a humming sound when placed on a unique turntable. Supposedly, in 1974, Austrian engineer named Ernst Wegener visited Banpo Museum in Xi'an, Shaanxi, where he saw two of the Dropa stones. He inquired about the discs but received no information, but he was allowed to take one in his hand and photograph them up close.

"By 1994, the discs could no longer be found. All governments involved have denied the existence of such disks. The original rendition of the story as it appeared in *Das vegetarische Universum* was credited to Reinhardt Wegemann, although no German writer with this name can be found. The article cites a DINA news agency in Tokyo which has disappeared and has left no trace. DINA is a cloud-based newsroom and storytelling tool that allows users to plan, create, and publish stories in one unified tool. It runs in a browser from anywhere, enables collaboration, and publishes to any platform. Outside of subsequent retellings of the tale of the Dropa stones, no mention has been found of Chu PuTei or Tsum Um Nui or of their academic work. It has also been suggested that he is not an authentic Chinese person, having never existed.

"There seems to be a widespread cover-up to conceal the existence of the Dropa disks, and I believe One World Order is behind it all. When we were in the astral plane, Koka made contact with the energy of the curator of Banpo Museum, who had the Dropa disks and passed away shortly afterward. It turns out that after Austrian engineer Ernst Wegener visited Banpo Museum in 1974, he was ordered by his superior to destroy them immediately and report to him after doing so. The curator had an intuition and believed that they were crucial for humankind, so he decided to hide them instead.

"He went to the Neolithic excavations and to the building's store pit at the Banpo Neolithic Village. There, he found several pottery items, including a big jar with a lid. He placed them inside it and sealed the lid shut. He reported to his superior that it had been done, and later that night, he and his superior were abducted, executed, and disposed of secretly. He was thrilled to contact Koka, who could finally do something about it.

"You see, the beings that crashed were visiting the underground tunnels around the world, which were created to house and protect humans from the impending cataclysm, to leave instructions for survival, and to help them rebuild afterward. Also, they have information regarding the return of God and his angels. A lightning bolt hit their craft, and they lost power and crashed. This was recorded on the granite disks because they knew they could withstand the passage of time."

"Wow!" Thomas exclaimed. "So we will retrieve them and prove to the world the existence of God and his return. Do you have any idea of its significance and how it will change the perspective of our world and life itself?"

"Yes," replied Joe. "But there's more. While in the astral plane, Koka could sense another powerful being. He believes it was Satanail, who now knows about the disks and intends to prevent us from retrieving them."

Thomas continued, "Well then, there's no time to lose. I'm having James put together a plan. By the time you arrive at the Xi'an Xianyang International Airport in China, we'll have all the details for you, OK?"

"Yes, thank you," replied Ashlee.

"We also have information that would interest John, Luke, and Mathew. Would you like to hear it, guys?" Joe inquired.

"Of course," Mathew answered excitedly. "What is it?" So Ashlee told them that Koka was able to recover more consciousness and memories of his being and past. He allowed her to share it with them. She continued by telling them that Koka came from a world that's older than Earth and where life spontaneously appeared over one billion years ago. Many life forms evolved and went extinct until approximately our million years ago, during which the current life form was created. They were visited by the superior being, who created our universe and seeded life throughout it. They don't know his true form because he's mostly a powerful energy being, who's existed since before time and whom they refer to as, "The Most High." He created their civilization, starting with male and female beings, which people may know as Anu and Ki.

"I'm using the names given by the ancient Earth civilizations so you can relate to them. Their offspring, the Anunnaki, are also known as the Egyptian gods, the Greek gods, Yahweh and his legion of angels, the Sacred Dragon, etc. Their names varied depending on the civilizations, but they were the same: one and only gods. The Most High communicates telepathically with them and is committed to helping them continue evolving until they reach their higher form," Ashlee said.

Luke blurted out," Wow! I suspected something like that. It's incredible." Mathew and John both agreed.

Ashlee continued telling Koka's story. "They lived in a world much larger than Earth and with more gravity, so their bodies are four to five meters tall or more, with strong bone structures, incredible strength, and increased mental abilities. They live fifty to sixty thousand years and are technologically advanced. Even so, it takes them several thousands of years to travel from their planet to ours. They are in a red dwarf solar system, and their atmosphere has become very unstable, exposing them to dangerously higher cosmic radiation levels.

"They can stabilize and even reverse it by increasing their electromagnetic field, which is weakening but can be boosted using gold. Unfortunately, their world is depleting its supply of gold, and they now have to explore other planets to find deposits worth mining. The Most High gave them the knowledge to find and travel to Earth, where there were large deposits of gold. At the time, Earth was populated with primitive life-forms, who didn't interfere with mining operations—"

"God sent them to our planet?" John said, interrupting.

Ashlee replied, "Yes, they journeyed to our world in enormously huge vessels with advanced propulsion systems. They were full of equipment, supplies, and personnel, both Anunnaki and the workers, who were called Igigi. They were the younger beings whom the Anunnaki created to be servants; they were half humanoid and half animals. They were semi-intelligent, and it's their spirits that modern humankind calls demons.

"Over five hundred million years ago, life appeared on Earth and evolved from single cells to complex life-forms of many diverse species. Some of them dominated others, but all were of low intelligence and had basic instincts. Humankind's ancestor, Homo erectus, was the species in existence at the time. This was the situation when approximately 450,000 years ago, space travelers, the Anunnaki, while exploring the universe discovered our planet Earth. They were accompanied by another alien race they had encountered in their exploration. They had small, fragile bodies but also high intelligence. They were also interested in exploring and had proven very helpful to the Anunnaki."

Mathew exclaimed, "Oh, my God! There was more than one alien species?"

Ashlee answered, "Yes, they were interested in the resources of our planet, especially gold, which they needed to continue space exploration of the universe, our galaxy, and the solar system. They established an outpost here, which would supply their spacecraft with fuel and other essential supplies needed in their quest during stopovers. This outpost was one of their space vessels, which was several miles in diameter and over a mile high in its center. When they landed just beyond but in front of the Pillars of Hercules, as the strait of Gibraltar was to be known later on, it seemed to bridge the distance from one coast to the other."

"This wouldn't by any chance be the Greek mythology legend of Atlantis, the lost continent?" asked Luke.

Ashlee smiled and replied, "Yes. At that time, the ocean levels were much lower, giving the illusion that the craft was a circular island with a mountain. The island of Atlas or Atlantis as the Greeks later referred to it regarded it as the domain of Poseidon, the god of the sea. In Greek mythology, Atlas supported the pillars that held heaven and Earth apart, and he was the son of the Titan Iapetus and the Oceanid Clymene and the brother of Prometheus, creator of humankind. These were all names given later on to the Anunnaki, who were perceived as gods."

"Incredible," exclaimed John.

"That's not all," continued Ashlee. "Their home planet was becoming rapidly insufficient to support them in overcoming diseases and prolonging life by many thousands of years. Their mission was to explore and colonize worlds throughout the universe that could be suitable for them. In the meantime, they would be mining for the gold needed to stabilize the atmosphere back on their own planet. These beings had evolved physically and mentally into highly advanced life-forms, who were well adapted to their planet and space exploration but were unsuitable for living in our planet's decreased gravity and extreme terrain conditions. They had their workers, the Igigi, doing the majority of the heavy labor for thousands of years.

"But the Igigi got tired of the hard labor and rebelled against the dictatorship of Enlil, who was the king at the time. They set fire to their tools and surrounded Enlil's great house that night. On hearing the reason for the discontent, the Anunnaki council decided that they would be replaced by creating a local species who would be more suitable to carry out manual labor. They needed help mining certain minerals, such as gold and uranium, and harvesting Earth's resources."

John said, "So it's true then; we were created?"

Ashlee took a deep breath and replied, "It does seem that way. They genetically modified primitive species found on Earth that were physically strong and well adapted to the harsh conditions. They had poor results in the beginning. They had been using several different types of earth animals, infusing them with their own DNA and creating uncontrollable and unreliable hybrids. However, after many attempts, they succeeded in evolving a primitive primate. The Homo erectus was genetically modified with their DNA into an intelligent species, who could follow commands and have the necessary dexterity to do their work. They created the Neanderthals, Denosovans, and other similar branches approximately 350,000 years ago.

"They were taught skills and an understanding of their surroundings to make them more productive for manual labor. This worked for some time, but the Neanderthals were very short-tempered and hostile. Enki, with permission from the council, proceeded to enhance the Homo erectus species by using his own DNA until he was successful in creating Homo sapiens, modern humankind, approximately 150,000 years ago. Population centers flourished in several continents, especially in fertile lands along rivers, lakes, or seas, such as the Mediterranean basin, where the conditions were best for survival and reproduction."

Mathew said," Well we always knew God created us, so I guess in a way this confirms it."

Ashlee said, "To make sure their creations would survive, these space visitors also gave humankind the knowledge of agriculture, farming, building, etc., so that they could learn to feed and shelter themselves and thrive in their new environment. With help from the sky beings, advanced civilizations formed in what are now Egypt, Mesopotamia, the Hindu Valley, the Yellow River valley in China, and Mesoamerica. This would always ensure enough manual labor for the demands of the work of the Anunnaki, or sky beings as they were being called at that time by humankind. With the help of the sky beings, many megalithic structures and pyramids were built by humans throughout the world and at other mining outposts, as markers for space travelers and time trackers for humankind."

Joe said, "Many of the outposts established throughout the planet were at locations where energy and electromagnetic fields made it easier to travel back and forth between the orbiting mother ship and Earth bases. They were using energy transportation machines to teleport, moving instantaneously from one location to another without physically occupying the space in between, transferring matter, such as beings and objects—including themselves—or energy from one point to another without traversing the physical space between them. Many of them were at mountaintops, high plateaus, where the energy lines crossed each other, and the concentration of energy was more intense.

"Most travels were done using the energy teleportation gateways, and smaller spacecraft were used to commute between bases or for local exploration. They used thought projection and holographic images to communicate among themselves and with humans. Many sky beings who were stationed in the outposts became so fond of Earth women that they decided to breed with them, having offspring that contained part of the sky beings. They were bigger and stronger. Some had elongated heads like their creators, and they were more intelligent than ordinary humans."

Luke said, "So the myths of demigods, such as Hercules, Samson, giants, and the Nephilim are true?"

Joe replied, "Yes, not only are they true but also these mixed beings were placed in command as kings of human population centers and human workers in the outposts. This relationship was very effective for the sky beings' purposes for thousands of years. Humankind gradually became more aware of its situation. With an increased mental and physical capability, which humans were rapidly acquiring from interbreeding and normal evolution, they started questioning the role and destiny that the sky beings had assigned to him. This became a divisive issue with the sky beings, some of whom favored continuing the same relationship with humankind while others wanted this to stop and to eliminate all humans, especially those with the sky beings' genetic material, which threatened their mission and future."

John said, "So we were spared?"

Joe answered, "Well, yes, but first an extensive and terrible war in the heavens ensued between both factions of the sky beings. They used incredible and powerful weapons, which humankind had never seen before. This war was won by the faction opposing humankind's increased capability. The sky beings that had bred with them were expelled and exiled to Earth. They were later referred to by humankind as fallen angels. The time when the gods walked among humans had ended, and a plan to terminate humankind was in motion.

"But first, the Anunnaki sky beings or messengers of the Most High, who were later referred to by humans as the Greek translated word *angels*, had to get his approval. Upon the creation of the universe with its galaxies and solar systems, the Most High or YHWH as he was later referred to by humankind, established a system of astral planes surrounding all planets with life-forms. This was to capture, store,

116

and reuse the cosmic energy of all living beings which constantly underwent cycles of birth and death to increase the level of energy and enlightenment of the astral cosmic consciousness like a dynamo. At the end of time, the fate of the cosmic energy stored in each planet's astral plane will be decided.

"Later on, Enoch was given the ability to visit and witness the different levels of the astral planes so that he could write about them and warn humankind. In his apocryphal book, Enoch wrote about Mount Hermon being the place where the watcher class of fallen angels descended to Earth. It's where they swore upon the mountain that they would take wives among the daughters of humans and responsibility for their sins. It was also how he witnessed the fallen angels residing in the different astral planes of Earth and heaven waiting for the end of time. All the stories and myths from the Sumerians, Egyptians, Greeks, Romans, Chinese, and the Vedas from India are all the same and true."

"That's incredible! Since the findings at Göbekli Tepe, we now know we're not alone in the universe, but this is so much more. It will rewrite history and redefine our world and social structure," Mathew exclaimed in excitement.

"Yes, but here's the more important part of the story," Joe said. "With the approval of YHWH, the Anunnaki or Earth gods, using their advanced technology, captured and sent an asteroid toward Earth. As we already know, it fragmented into thousands of pieces. It exploded over North America twelve thousand years ago, melting the glaciers and causing a severe worldwide flood and the resurgence of the ice age for another thousand years. The Anunnaki left Earth and abandoned their settlements, soon to be destroyed by the cataclysm that was on its way.

"Several of the exiled sky beings or fallen angels asked the Most High for mercy on humankind for the good of the righteous among them, and he did. They were allowed to select the Earth creatures to be saved from the impending disaster. They were also permitted to guide and help humankind rebuild their civilization and continue to evolve to the end of time. They proceeded to help the humans build boats or arks to survive the initial worldwide flooding and construct underground shelters to protect them from the resurgence of the ice age, with the severe freezing temperatures that would follow."

With a somber voice, Luke said, "So the world flood did happen, it wasn't natural, and humankind almost went extinct?"

Joe said, "Yes, but with help from the sky beings humans remained underground until the surface conditions improved, which it did after a thousand years. These fallen angels, including the one we know as Kokabiel, went all over the world, establishing storage compartments inside caves and tunnels where they hid knowledge inscribed on materials that would withstand the passage of time and adverse conditions. This would be needed to help humankind survive and rebuild its civilization because by then, the sky beings or angels would no longer be alive to help. But most important, they documented the covenant that the Most High had made with humankind and information regarding his return with his legions of angels and of our fate. This is what's on the Dropa disks that we are going to China to retrieve, and it's crucial for our existence that we get there before One World Order."

"It all makes sense now. We suspected all the ancient civilizations' gods were just different versions of the same. We served them once, and afterward, they tried getting rid of us, but we survived. Can we do it again?" Luke inquired.

"You bet," answered John. "The key is to find those caches of data they hid, which have instructions, and with Koka helping us, we can do it."

Thomas said, "Well, that's great because One World Order has activated its followers worldwide. There are increasing riots in all major cities of every country and what seem to be coordinated efforts to destabilize their governments. There's also growing hostility between many countries, which are threatening war. It appears that they have stepped up their efforts to take control amid the chaos, unhappiness, drought, starvation, and pandemics plaguing us, which are augmented with the uncertainty of governments not knowing what to do. The OWO seems to know something will happen soon, and I don't like it. We need to find out what it is and when this is going down and try to stop it."

Always ready with a plan of action, James said, "We can start by retrieving those Dropa disks. I have Ashlee and Joe's mission all planned and worked out. Two of our agents will meet them at the Xi'an Xianyang International Airport in Shaanxi, China, and they will assist and drive you to your destination. In the meantime, I suggest we all sleep because tomorrow will be hectic." Everyone agreed.

Ashlee and Joe sat beside each other in the back of the jet with their lights dimmed. Joe mentally said to Mia, "Turn off my communicator to everyone but Ashlee." He turned to gaze at Ashlee, and without even saying or thinking a word, he knew what she was thinking. Since the last astral plane session, he felt this intense attraction and warm feeling toward Ashlee. He could sense that she was experiencing the same thing. He could sense an increased connection of their minds and thoughts between them.

***

Ashlee gave Mia a thought command to keep her conversation with Joe private. Ashlee then projected her thoughts reluctantly. "Joe, can you hear me?"

"Yes," he answered, smiling at her tenderly. "I know what you're going to ask me. I, too, feel the same way." He confirmed her thoughts as he grabbed and held her hand, squeezing it. Ashlee felt her cheeks flush with color, yet she returned his smile and entwined her fingers with his. "The merging of our souls in the astral plane seems to have left some of us in each other, even when we're back in our bodies. I now know what it means to have someone in your heart," Joe said.

She gave him a soft look. "I think love was an unexpected side effect that we didn't count on. As much as I enjoy this feeling, we should try not to let it get in the way of our mission; we'll deal with it later." She frowned, pursing her lips. Putting their newly discovered feelings on hold was painful.

Yet Joe raised their joined hands and rested them against his chest, and Ashlee found herself smiling at the gesture. "I know. But the minute we're through, you're mine. Rest for now, and I'll let you know when we're there." Ashlee blushed with a grin before turning, closing her eyes, and falling sleep.

CHAPTER FIFTEEN

BANPO MUSEUM

Joe breathed in the cool air-conditioned air of the aircraft after he woke and before turning his head and looking at Ashlee sleeping soundly beside him. A deep sense of affection warmed him from within, and he leaned closer, tucking some wayward strands behind her ear and away from her face. In slumber, she looked all the more beautiful. There was an innocence about her that was subdued in her waking hours. It would be a lie to deny that he didn't find her beautiful before merging their souls. However, since the merging, he had also begun to notice all the little things that he had previously overlooked before.

More than that, though, he had started to feel something that he had never felt for any woman before, and it was a beautiful sensation. The way his pulse quickened in awareness of her closeness and the zing of sparks he felt through his nerve endings every time they touched were thrilling. He couldn't wait to explore this bond further. He wondered if their merging would continue with every astral projection and how it would affect their feelings for each other.

An approaching flight attendant broke him out of his thoughts, and he gestured for her to leave. He wanted to be the one to wake Ashlee first. Gently, he touched her shoulder and caressed her arm while speaking softly to rouse her. "Hey, wake up. We're here." She blinked sleepily, met his gaze, and gave him a tender smile that made his heart melt.

"Hey," she rasped.

"Hey," he replied with a smile in return.

She broke eye contact and sat up. He leaned back in his seat, knowing that this little moment was over—for now. "Thank you," she said softly.

The flight attendant returned and announced, "We will arrive at our destination in ten minutes. Please prepare for landing."

Just then, James came online and said, "Hello, guys. Thomas wants me to go over the plan with you."

"OK," they both answered.

He said, "It's midnight here in Xi'an and a comfortable 56 degrees Fahrenheit, which should help the mission go slightly smoother. Two agents of ours will be waiting at the airport. They will help you get through customs and immigration quickly. You are posing as visiting representatives for a large investment group interested in doing business in China. They have a car and the tools necessary for your mission, and they will assist you in every way possible. They don't know what the target is but only the location: Banpo Museum. They will drive you there. It takes approximately thirty-eight minutes, and traffic should be light at this hour. Once you retrieve the disks, you will return to the airport, and hopefully, we'll be out of here and back on international waters in three to four hours max and before anyone can sound the alarm. Do you have any questions?"

They smiled, and Joe answered, "No, it sounds pretty straightforward."

The jet door opened, and Joe and Ashlee entered a cool, breezy, and beautiful night. The two shared a glance, and Ashlee knew they would come back here once everything was said and done. They went down the stairway, and at the bottom, they were met by two men. One of them said, "Hi! We're with the Group. I'm Chen." Pointing to the other man, he said, "This is Chang. We'll help you get through the authorities, and then we'll be on our way, OK?"

"Excellent," answered Joe. They followed the two men, who spoke to the Chinese officials, and a few minutes later, they were given a welcome-to-China greeting. The four of them entered the parking lot and got into a new Mercedes S550.

Mia came online. "Hello, I will monitor your route and the hold time and alert you to anything wrong. Your driver was provided with the route. It was programmed in the car's navigational system."

"Thank you, Mia," Ashlee answered with a thought.

The ride to the museum was uneventful, and thirty-eight minutes later, Chen announced, "We're here."

"Mia, give me a mental image of the map for this place," Ashlee instructed. The four proceeded to go directly to the building with the Neolithic excavations.

Once there, Joe turned to Chang. "You stand guard here at the door and watch our backs. We won't be long."

The three then proceeded to go to the excavation and searched until they located the storage pit. Ashlee and Joe went up to the jar with a lid. Ashlee offered her palm to Chen and said, "Pass us the bag of tools." They then pried open the jar lid with metal chisels and removed it. Ashlee looked inside with a flashlight and silently gasped. "Oh my God, they're here." She reached in and pulled out the first and then a second disk.

Ashlee took photos of the disks with her cellphone. Joe then turned to Chen. "Go ahead and seal the jar again. We don't want any unnecessary attention." While Chen placed the lid on the jar, Joe put the disks in a backpack. Once done, they headed for the door. Upon arriving there, they saw Chang lying on the floor, unconscious. The three quickly became alert. "Fan out. Five to six persons are lingering outside," Joe hissed.

Mia answered instantly. "Six people are hiding in the bushes. I will provide you with their thermal images and locations."

Joe turned to the other two. With urgency in his words, he said, "When I launch my plasma ball, both of you attack the four on my left. I'll take care of these two on my right." He formed a giant plasma ball, flung it onto the person farthest on his right, and yelled, "Go!" They launched a coordinated attack and got the upper hand on the agents of OWO.

Ashlee confronted two of them with her thought-reading abilities. Using her martial art moves and blows, she defeated and disabled two enemy agents. She went to help Chen, who was having trouble with the two he was fighting. As Ashlee helped Chen, she started to dominate them, as if she could guess their movements and counteract them with her own fist, arm, and leg blows. Chen marveled at her fighting ability, saying to her," Ashlee, I'm a martial arts' expert, and I can appreciate your incredible power."

Ashlee replied, "Thank you, Chen." After defeating their enemies, they went to look for Joe, whom they found fighting not one or two but four enemy agents. After knocking one of them unconscious with his plasma ball, three more had showed up, but thanks to Mia alerting him, he had been able to fight them off. One of them managed to take his backpack and run away with it. With Ashlee and Chen's help, they were able to defeat the enemy agents in no time at all.

Joe then yelled, "Let's go after the backpack. The person who took it ran toward the main entrance." They ran him, but just as they were almost there, several gunmen showed up and started firing at them with automatic weapons. Chen returned fire while Joe formed another plasma ball and fired it at them, temporarily blinding them and allowing Ashlee to reach and attack them with lightning-fast moves.

Joe joined her. Soon while using flying kicks, hand and fist blows, and martial arts' moves, they were able to dominate and defeat the agents. "Mia, where's the backpack with the disks? It had a tracker, didn't it?" Ashlee asked.

Mia answered, "I don't know. I was able to track it after it left the museum and got into a car, but then they got on the G3002 freeway going south, and the signal disappeared. I believe they found the tracking device, or it's in a shielded vehicle. I can no longer track it."

"OK," said Joe. "Let's get Chang and head back to the airport." They got Chang, who was finally coming to, and headed for the airport, where they arrived shortly afterward. Ashlee and Joe thanked Chen and Chang, got into their jet, and took off. Once in the air, Thomas and everyone else came online and welcomed them back.

Thomas said, "I'm sorry and sad that they took the disks, but we are all thrilled you're alive and well." They heard everyone concur with him.

"Thank you, everyone, but what do we do now?" Joe asked.

Thomas answered, "Well, for now, come home, and we'll try and figure out our next move. In the meantime, you get some rest, and I'll get back to you hopefully before you reach home."

Ashlee bit her lip. "There's one more thing, guys. I was shot when we were at Banpo Museum. I didn't say anything because I thought it was a superficial flesh wound, but now I'm not so sure." Feeling lightheaded, Ashlee then turned to Joe. "I don't feel good," she said and then lost consciousness.

Trembling, Joe's eyes widened in shock and terror as he exclaimed, "Ashlee, what's wrong?" And then he noticed blood on her left side.

Mia spoke up. "She has a gunshot wound; the bullet went through and out her left flank."

With mounting panic, Joe asked, "Will she be OK? She feels very cold, and I can't wake her up."

"She's lost a lot of blood, probably from internal bleeding. Her vital signs are very weak. I'm sorry, Joe, but nothing can be done. The aircraft doesn't have the equipment to explore the wound and stop the bleeding," Mia answered.

All of a sudden, Ashlee made a gasping sound and stopped breathing. Joe broke down. "No, please, Ashlee! Don't die on me." He hugged her body and started sobbing, visibly shaken. The thought of not having Ashlee in his life was unbearable. While Joe was being consumed with grief, he began hearing an internal voice that was urging him to take her right hand with his and place it over the wound. It took him a few seconds to realize that Koka was contacting and instructing him what to do. Joe placed her hand with his over the wound. As he concentrated on this area of her body, he could feel tremendous energy flowing to Ashlee. Suddenly, the gunshot wound started to glow, and gradually, it began to heal until all traces of it disappeared.

Then Ashlee took a deep breath and opened her eyes. "Oh God," Joe cried out, "you're alive!" and started laughing and hugging her even as tears leaked from his eyes, this time from immense relief. It had become clear in his mind that he wanted to spend his life with Ashlee, and he would do whatever he needed to protect her and to provide a safe world for her—by eliminating One World Order.

Ashlee pulled back slightly, cupped his face with her hands, and wiped his tears with the pads of his thumbs. Her face was soft and regretful. "I'm sorry I gave you such a scare. I didn't believe my injury was that bad, and I didn't say anything to not worry you."

Thomas and the rest of the team sighed in relief, and then he said, "You had all of us scared to death. Welcome back. Your recovery was just amazing."

Ashlee smiled. "Well, it was a combined effort between Joe, Koka, and my healing abilities."

Thomas said, "Now that everyone is well, and things are back on track, try and get some rest during your flight home."

Joe picked her up and placed her in her seat. Kneeling, he kissed her forehead. Staring briefly into her eyes, he whispered, "Please don't do that again."

"I won't."

Joe got into his own seat. They reclined, grasping onto each other's hands. Soon, they were sound asleep.

★★★

Ashlee and Joe woke up suddenly and at the same time. Ashlee spoke up. "We know what to do." After discussing their dream, they proceeded to share it with the team, which had just come online. Koka had contacted them while they were asleep. He told them that the beings who crashed in China with the Dropa stones were an advanced party of a larger group, who was doing the same thing in other parts of the world.

Joe then said, "If we can enter the astral plane, maybe Koka can make contact with the cosmic energy of these beings and find out if there are other hidden stones."

"That's great! Let's get on with it," Thomas replied. Ashlee and

Joe sat back-to-back in the back of the plane. Soon after achieving total meditation relaxation as they had done many times before, they opened a gateway above their heads. With a sudden loud noise and bright light, they passed into the astral plane and found themselves in their pure-energy bodies.

Koka found them almost immediately. "It feels great being here with you both, but we have more work to do. I can feel the energy of the beings who were delivering the stones flowing around me. They're trying to communicate with me, so I need to concentrate on their energy." As they were moving through the astral plane and were immersed in the cosmic energy, they felt Koka searching for the beings' energy. After a few minutes, Koka said, "I got it. We can leave now." But before Ashlee and Joe could pull in the silver cord, Koka exclaimed, "Wait, not yet. There's another energy being like us in here, and it's evil."

All of a sudden, a pure-energy body appeared close to them, and they heard a malevolent voice. "That's not nice to say about someone you don't know."

Koka seemed angered. "You're wrong; I do know you. Ashlee and Joe, let me introduce you to Satan."

"Now, Brother, there's no need for us to fight against each other. We should be on the same side." Satan sounded completely at ease, arrogant, and with an undercurrent of deviousness in his tone.

"That will never happen. You want to destroy this world and challenge the Most High. I want to help the humans honor their covenant with our Father," Koka declared.

Immediately, Satan became disgruntled, and his voice turned menacing. "Then I will destroy you and your friends. Father and you will not stop me from my destiny to rule this world." Using his hands, he launched a red energy beam at Koka with the sound of thunder. Koka felt the impact, and he lost some of his strength afterward. This weakening was felt by Joe and Ashlee. Koka then used his hands to launch an energy beam at Satan, who used an energy field to deflect it. Satan just laughed and attacked again. Koka was able to dodge the red lightning beam, but he knew it wouldn't last. Koka attempted to strike Satan with energy beams, but they were too weak to cause any damage.

"Koka, what's the problem? Isn't our energy body as strong as his?" Ashlee questioned.

Koka sounded helpless. "I'm afraid not. His energy body is one being—him—and he can navigate the astral plane himself or enter his physical body at will. In either plane, he can control his body without any external help. We are three beings combined into one, which causes gaps in our cosmic energy body."

Joe frowned contemplatively. "So is he subject to the weaknesses that one being has?"

"What do you mean?" Koka asked.

"Well, I can help you generate a much stronger energy weapon: the plasma ball. Ashlee can help read his thoughts so we can anticipate his movements and counter them. Between the three of us, we have an advantage over him. Let us use it, OK?"

Koka slowly nodded. "You may be right. With the three of us working together, we just might pull it off. Let's give it a go." Koka attacked Satan again, but this time while working with Joe, they conjured up a plasma ball and launched it with all the power they could generate. Satan tried blocking it again with his shield, but the impact penetrated and struck him this time. Satan felt the debilitating effect but immediately tried launching another bolt of energy at Koka.

This time, Ashlee successfully read his thoughts, and with her help, Koka evaded the impact, and he was able to send another plasma ball at Satan. After this impact, Satan decided that he had had enough. He quickly left and disappeared, most likely back to his physical body.

"Yeah!" all three cheered.

"Now we know that we can even beat the devil when working together," Ashlee boasted. They laughed and proceeded to return to their physical bodies.

As soon as they had returned to their bodies, Joe asked, "Hey, guys, is everyone online?"

Thomas answered instantly, "Yes, we are, and we have some news, but we wanted to know how it went in the astral plane."

"It went great! We'll fill you in, but first, what news do you have?" Ashlee said.

Luke answered, "Remember the photos Ashlee took of the Dropa disks with her cell phone? Well Mia retrieved them and was able to reconstruct the surface of the disks from the photos. Then we had our cryptology department work on them to decipher the writings. The writing is the same unknown ancient language we found on the artifacts we recovered from Father Crespi in Ecuador and the relics from Göbekli Tepe. They're instructions on what to do to survive the cataclysm they were expecting at that time. They reminded people to observe the covenant they had made with the Most High until the end of time. It also stated that they had just distributed the stone messages to another underground shelter they had built in the land, just before crossing the vast body of water."

CHAPTER SIXTEEN

THE HOPI

John elaborated further. "All of us have been working nonstop for many hours since you left China to make sense of what we deciphered and to come up with an answer or location. I believe we found what we were looking for, so I'm going to start with some background information."

John proceeded to brief them on the information they had uncovered. He told them, "Twenty thousand years ago, people settled in the deep canyons of present-day New Mexico. The members of these ancient civilizations—the ancestral Puebloans who were also known as the Anasazi—the Mogollon, and the Hohokam built cities carved into the cliffs. Almost all of them created complex canals to water crops in the desert.

"The southwestern tribes, who later spread out into regions we know as present-day Arizona, Texas, and northern Mexico, can trace their ancestry back to these civilizations. The Hopi's sacred land, the Four Corners area where Arizona, New Mexico, Colorado, and Utah meet, was called Tukunavi. It is part of the heart of our Mother Earth. The Hopi have a fascinating story of creation, which is very similar to that of the Sumerians and other civilizations—"

"OK, I imagine this has something to do with the Dropa disks?" Joe interrupted.

John replied, "Yes, let me continue. The Hopi creation story centers on Tawa, the sun spirit. Tawa is the creator, and he formed the first world out of Tokpella or endless space, as well as its original inhabitants. Tawa first created Sotuknang, whom he called his nephew, and sent him to create the nine universes according to his plan. Sotuknang created SpiderWoman, who served as a messenger for the Creator and was an intercessor between the Creator, him, and the people. She also creates all life under the direction of Sotuknang, while the sun spirit merely observes the process.

"According to Hopi legend, when time and space began, after the sun spirit (Tawa) created the first world, he also created insect-like creatures that lived unhappily in caves. With the goal of improvement, Tawa sent a spirit called Spider Grandmother to the world below. Spider Grandmother led the first creatures on a long trip to the second world, in which they appeared as wolves and bears. As these animals were no happier than the previous ones, Tawa created a new third world and again sent Spider Grandmother to convey the wolves and bears there. By the time they arrived, they had become people.

"Spider Grandmother taught them weaving, pottery, and other skills. The people there became wicked, so Tawa destroyed the third world in a great flood. Before the destruction, Spider Grandmother sealed the more righteous people into hollow reeds used as boats. On arriving at a small piece of dry land, the people saw nothing around them but more water, even after planting a large bamboo shoot, climbing to the top, and looking about. Spider Woman then told the people to make boats out of more reeds. Using islands as stepping stones along the way, the people sailed east until they arrived on the mountainous coasts of the fourth world."

"Wow!" Ashlee exclaimed. "That sounds so similar to Noah's flood."

John replied, "That's not all. In this fourth world, the people learned many lessons about how to live properly. They learned to worship Masauwu, who ensured that the dead returned safely to the underworld and gave them the four sacred tablets, which in symbolic form outlined their wanderings and proper behavior in the fourth world. Masauwu also told the people to watch for the Pahána, the lost, white brother. In Hopi mythology, the skeleton man or Masauwu is regarded as the lord of the dead. He is the one who taught the people about the importance of agriculture. Although his appearance can be frightening, he is regarded as a good friend of humans and can be trusted to look after the Hopi people.

"One of the most intriguing Hopi legends involves the ant people, who were crucial to the survival of the Hopi—not just once but twice. First, the world was apparently destroyed by fire. It was possibly some sort of asteroid strike followed by worldwide flooding. Then the world was destroyed a second time by ice age glaciers approximately twelve thousand years ago. During these two global cataclysms, the virtuous members of the Hopi tribe were guided by an odd-shaped cloud during the day and a moving star at night, which led them to the sky god named Sotuknang, who finally took them to the ant people; in Hopi, it's Anu Sinom."

Joe said, "That sounds familiar like when the Hebrew tribes were led out of Egypt."

John replied, "The ant people then escorted the Hopi into subterranean caves, where they found refuge and sustenance for many generations. In this legend, the ant people are portrayed as generous and industrious, giving the Hopi food when supplies ran short and teaching them the merits of food storage. It is interesting to note that the Babylonian sky god was named Anu. The Hopi word for *ant* is also *anu*, and the Hopi root word *naki* means friends. Thus, the Hopi Anu-Naki or ant friends may have been the same as the Sumerian Anunnaki—the beings who once came to Earth from the heavens.

"The ant people may have also lived in ancient Egypt. Akhenaten, the eighteenth dynasty pharaoh who ruled from 1351–1334 BC, is shown in some depictions with an elongated skull like the shape of an ant's head. His almond-shaped eyes and neck are like the ants are. Either the serpent or the vulture on his uraeus resembles the ant's mandibles. He also has spindly arms and legs like an ant, and his upper body resembles the ant's thorax, while his lower body mirrors the ant's abdomen.

"Akhenaten's body type can be compared explicitly to the pharaoh ant, which originated in West Africa. It also has an elongated head, a yellow-to-reddish-brown body, and a darker abdomen with a stinger. Perhaps it is more than a coincidence that the Egyptian word *sahu* means stars of Orion, whereas the Hopi word *sohu* means star, the most important of which are those in the constellation Orion. So the ant people and the Hopi have a connection to ancient Egypt.

"After many generations, the ant people guided the survivors back to the surface. They were instructed to divide into three groups and go east, west, south, but not north. Far in the north was a land of snow and ice called the back door, but this was closed to the Hopi. However, the Hopi say that other people, probably the Clovis, came through the back door into the fourth world. The back door could refer to the Bering land bridge, which connected Asia with North America. The survivors were led on their migrations by various signs or were helped along by SpiderWoman.

"The Hopi clans finished their prescribed migrations and were led to their current location in northeastern Arizona. Most Hopi traditions have it that Masauwu, the spirit of death and master of the fourth world, gave them their land. Hopi tradition tells of sacred tablets imparted to the Hopi by various deities. Accounts differ regarding when the tablets were given and in what manner. Perhaps the most important sacred tablet was said to have been in the possession of the Fire Clan, and it is related to the return of the Pahana, the white-beard brother, who had helped them rebuild after they emerged to the surface. When he returns from the East, an elder of the Fire Clan, who was worried that his people would not recognize the Pahana, broke off a corner piece from a stone tablet to help identify him.

"This section was given to Pahana. He was told to bring it back with him so that a witch or sorcerer would not deceive the Hopi. The true Pahana is the lost white brother of the Hopi or elder brother who left for the East at the time when the Hopi entered the fourth world and began their migrations. He probably was one of the Anunnaki gods. However, the Hopi say that he will return, and at his coming, the wicked will be destroyed, and a new age of peace, the fifth world, will be ushered in.

"The above-mentioned Kachinas Pahana will bring with him the missing section of the sacred Hopi stone tablet in the possession of the Fire Clan, and he will come wearing red. The legend of the Pahana seems intimately connected with the Aztec story of Quetzalcoatl and other legends of Central America. This similarity is furthered by the liberal representation of Awanyu or the Paluliikon, the horned or plumed serpent found in Hopi and other Puebloan art. This figure also resembles Quetzalcoatl, the feathered serpent of Mexico. In the early sixteenth century, both the Hopis and the Aztecs believed that the coming of the Spanish conquistadors was the return of this lost white-brother prophet. But the Hopi found out that they weren't because they put the Spaniards to the test, which they failed."

Thomas spoke up next. "So we believe a stone tablet exists somewhere in the southwest of the United States, which can shed light on the sky beings and their possible return. We just don't know where to look, but we're working on it."

Ashlee smiled. "Well, we do. As a matter of fact, let me fill you in on what happened when we were in the astral plane." Ashlee told them everything that had happened and about their success in gathering information. She elaborated on how they managed to make contact with the beings, who were delivering the stones, and how they disclosed the location of the sacred tablet given to the Hopi, which had the information regarding the return of Pahana, the sky being. And finally, she told of how they had battled Satan and had defeated him.

"So your information and ours confirm the existence of a sacred tablet with the information on it, which will hopefully help us defeat OWO and save Earth," Joe said.

"Great!" Thomas said in a somber voice before continuing. "Because the world is going mad, countries are on the verge of war with one another, and governments can't seem to stop the violent protesting and rioting in all major cities, which seem to have the goal of destabilizing civil order and toppling the authorities. So do you know where we go next so I can give the pilots their new flight plan?"

"Yes, we're going back to where we started: Arizona—more specifically, to Flagstaff," Ashlee said.

"OK, I will give the pilots their new destination," Thomas said.

Joe spoke up then. "There's something more you guys should know. As it turns out, this ancient Hopi myth is actually true. The *katsinam* are associated with clouds. They are benevolent supernatural entities and the spirits of all things in the universe—rocks, stars, animals, plants, and ancestors who have lived good lives. They inhabit San Francisco Mountain, just north of Flagstaff, Arizona. The Hopi believe that for six months of the year, Kachina spirits return and live in the Hopi villages.

"Kachina spirits taught them various forms of agriculture. The Hopi say that during a great drought, they heard singing and dancing from San Francisco Mountain. Upon investigation, they met the Kachinas, who returned with the Hopi to their villages to help them. The Hopi buried the sacred tablets there. The energy beings in the astral plane gave us the exact location: 35.315545 -111.707966. Did you get that, Mia?"

Mia answered, "Yes, I already plotted a navigational map from the Flagstaff airport to the exact location of the tablet. It will be available for you upon landing."

James said, "I will work out the details of your mission to San Francisco Mountain. In the meantime, I suggest you both get some rest. It will be several hours before you arrive." Joe and Ashlee agreed that they would. They then stretched out in their chairs and fell asleep while still holding hands.

THE CONFRONTATION

Ashlee and Joe were abruptly awakened by a sudden, violent jolt and vibrations that shook them to their cores. Startled and momentarily disoriented, they exchanged bewildered glances. Their minds raced to comprehend the situation. Just as they were about to voice their confusion, a flight attendant approached and urgently said, "We are under attack; please fasten your seat belts."

The pilot's voice crackled over the overhead speakers, cutting through the tension. He informed the passengers, "As we were flying over California, we came under attack by two unidentified fighter jets. We've sustained some damage, which is forcing us to make an emergency landing. I'm taking evasive maneuvers, so the ride may get a bit bumpy. We are descending, and I'm aiming to land at a small, abandoned airstrip in central California just a few miles ahead."

Mia's voice chimed in through their communication device, "Ashlee and Joe, agents of One World Order are targeting you. I intercepted their communications, and it appears they've launched a full-scale attack to halt your progress. I've analyzed the damage to your aircraft, and you should be able to land safely at the selected airstrip. Mary successfully hacked into the weapons system of the jets, disabling them. Unfortunately, I've detected four black SUVs in route to the same airstrip. It will take us at least forty-five minutes to reach you. Right now, two rescue helicopters are on their way. You have access to onboard weapons to defend yourselves and the crew." Grateful, Ashlee and Joe thanked Mia.

Once the aircraft safely touched down with a cacophonous roar, Joe wasted no time in shouting, "Everyone out. Let's make a run for that abandoned hangar. We have to quickly fortify our position. Search for anything we could use, such as sheets of metal, sand-filled sacks, and wood, OK?" They all scrambled into the building, finding wood tables, stacks of weathered paper bales, metal squares used for repair, and other construction material. Their improvised defenses were completed just in time. The OWO agents arrived in a flurry, leaping out of their vehicles while unleashing a hail of automatic gunfire.

Ashlee, Joe, the pilot, and the rest of the crew responded with a barrage of return fire. They wielded US military-issued firearms, specifically M4 and M4A1, 5.56-millimeter carbines—lightweight, gas-operated, air-cooled, magazine-fed, selective-fire weapons with collapsible stocks. Remarkably, the pilot, copilot, and flight attendants were military-trained personnel, a fact known to only a select few on board. Many of the Group's agents were either current or former armed forces members, who were exceptionally well-trained.

The firefight raged on, fierce and unrelenting. They held their ground against the onslaught of enemy agents, who seemed to multiply despite their successful eliminations. Recognizing a flanking maneuver by some of the OWO agents, Joe urgently sent a thought projection to Ashlee, directing her to cover the right flank. She acknowledged with, "Roger that," and swiftly moved into position. Joe instructed the crew to maintain their positions as he sprinted toward the left flank, determined to counter the threat.

***

Ashlee reached her position just as three enemy agents burst in through a side door. She swiftly engaged them, utilizing her martial arts' skills in the confines of close-quarters combat. The exchange of blows was relentless. Punches, flying kicks, and strikes with her fists and arms were met with counterattacks. In this intense battle, Ashlee's ability to anticipate her opponents' moves granted her a slight advantage and allowed her to overpower them gradually. She eliminated one of the agents with a well-executed combination of blows to the head and neck. Another adversary brandished a knife and relentlessly attempted to stab Ashlee. She sent a thought projection in a quick and calculated move, suggesting that he was being attacked from behind. In his confusion, he turned and inadvertently stabbed his own partner, believing it to be a genuine threat. Left with only one adversary, Ashlee easily dispatched him using a series of flying kicks.

★★★

Meanwhile, Joe had managed to overpower two enemy agents attempting to enter through a side door. He swiftly dispatched one with a gunshot and used his martial arts' prowess to eliminate the other. Exiting through the side door, he made his way to the front of the building, flanking the remaining enemy agents. Leveraging his ability to create plasma balls, he launched them methodically.

With the combined efforts of the flight crew's automatic fire and Ashlee's thought projections causing chaos among the agents, they successfully eliminated the remaining threats. As the dust settled, a tense silence enveloped the scene until the distant sound of approaching enemy jets shattered the calm. Joe exclaimed, "You've got to be kidding me; give us a break!"

Just as they prepared to assume defensive positions, a swooshing sound echoed through the air, followed by the spectacular sight of the first enemy jet exploding and then the second. Relief washed over them as they saw the Group's helicopters approaching. They all cheered in unison. Ashlee and Joe turned to the flight crew and expressed their gratitude, saying their thank-yous. The crew smiled and responded, "You're welcome."

Thomas voiced his relief, saying, "That was a close call. We're all so happy you're OK," as they heard the whole team cheering and expressing their relief.

In response, Joe replied, "It's not over. We can feel Koka calling us to the astral plane. Something important is happening, and we need to meet him there."

Thomas nodded understandingly. "All right, you two have your meeting, and by the time you're done, we should have a replacement aircraft ready to continue your flight to Flagstaff, Arizona."

With this plan in mind, Ashlee and Joe found a quiet, dimly lit back room. They sat down on the floor back-to-back and swiftly entered a state of total meditation and relaxation, which was a familiar practice. Opening a gateway above their heads, they transitioned into the astral plane with a sudden burst of loud noise and brilliant light. Here, they existed as pure energy in their astral bodies.

Koka's voice resonated in the astral realm. "We need to prepare ourselves for another attack. This time, the showdown will take place here in the astral plane. We are up against Satan again, but this time, he has enlisted some of his demons to assist him. I can sense them drawing nearer."

Ashlee inquired, "We understand Satan's strength, but how powerful are his demons, and how many of them are there?"

Koka replied, "There are only a few who are utterly loyal to him, such as Beelzebub, Asmodeus, Azael, Behemoth, and Bernael. Individually, their powers and abilities are limited. They are mostly effective within the astral plane rather than the physical world. However, when united, they can pose a significant challenge."

Joe inquired further. "What do they hope to achieve by attacking us within the astral plane where we can exit at will?"

Koka responded, "They are aware that if you exit, I would be left vulnerable and possibly unable to withstand their assault. This would leave you without my guidance to continue your quest in search of the ancient sacred tablets and to decipher their true significance and usage. It's a well-coordinated plan to halt your efforts in saving Earth."

Ashlee pressed for their plan of action, asking, "So what's the strategy? How are we going to handle this?"

Koka laid out their plan. "We are confident in our ability to defeat Satan. Our primary goal is to befuddle his demons and diminish their effectiveness in channeling energy to their leader. Ashley, you will need to delve into Satan's thoughts to help me evade his attacks and project confusing thoughts to his demons. Meanwhile, Joe will assail them with his plasma balls to weaken their resolve. Simultaneously, you must bolster my energy so we can launch an offensive against Satan."

With a resigned sigh, Ashlee agreed. "Well, no pressure at all. I guess we'll just have to do it."

Their discussion was interrupted by a booming voice. "It's good to see you again, Brother. I'm surprised you're not trying to evade me."

Koka calmly replied, "Why would I, Satan?"

Satan's reply came through Asmodeus. "Because today, dear Brother, you're not alone."

Koka retorted, "I see you still blindly follow without questioning right from wrong. Asmodeus, we pledged to follow Satan, but after our father's exile, you chose to stand behind our leader and prepare for the final battle." Koka explained that his plea to their father for mercy was not for himself but for the innocent humans who had no say in their actions. These humans were at risk of destruction due to their perceived danger simply because they had the misfortune of coexisting with them.

Suddenly, Satan hurled an energy bolt at Koka, but with Ashlee's assistance, he managed to evade it. Joe concentrated his energy into plasma balls, targeting the demons accompanying Satan. The thought projections from Ashlee caused confusion among the demons, rendering them incapable of assisting Satan effectively. Koka seized the opportunity to unleash energy bolts, which struck Satan with devastating force. Thunderous clashes of energy bolt accompanied by blinding flashes of intense light persisted for several minutes. Eventually, the demons weakened, and their energy faded. Satan, realizing their vulnerability, shouted, "Retreat!" With that, the battle concluded.

Ashlee, Joe, and Koka celebrated their victory, exclaiming that they had defeated him once more and this time, with his own demons. Ashlee declared it was time to leave, and they tugged on the silver cord.

Upon returning to their physical bodies, they exited the hangar and made their way to the waiting replacement jet. Thomas inquired, "Is everything OK? Are we still on track for the mission to Arizona?" They affirmed that everything was fine.

Joe added, "We had another encounter with Satan and some of his demons, but thanks to Koka, we devised a battle plan and emerged victorious. However, One World Order is clearly determined to stop us at any cost, so we must always remain vigilant."

Ashlee continued, "Also, we've learned more about our nemesis, One World Order. This knowledge comes to us whenever we cross one another's energy fields in the astral plane. Many hundreds of thousands of years ago, Satan and all the fallen angels, who went by different names at that time, rebelled and fought against the Creator and the rest of the gods. They desired to remain on Earth, which they claimed for themselves. They ruled over the humans, whom they considered their property and servants. This did not align with the Creator's intentions; the other gods recalled them to their celestial realms. A fierce battle ensued, but they were defeated and subsequently exiled to the astral plane as prisoners.

"The Creator and the other gods devised plans to eradicate the corrupted humans. Kokabiel, known by another name at that time, pleaded for mercy on behalf of the humans. He assured the Creator that not all of them were corrupt and that they were worth saving. He offered his own life in exchange. Touched by his sacrifice, the gods allowed him to rescue the righteous humans and appointed him to guide them in survival. He was tasked with conveying the message that upon the Creator's eventual return, they would face judgment. Their final fate would be determined by their actions. Koka dedicated himself to saving as many righteous humans as possible. He left them written instructions on how to endure and rebuild after the impending cataclysm while reminding them of their covenant with the Creator," Ashlee explained.

Joe added, "Furthermore, we now know that Satan has been recruiting followers for thousands of years and patiently placing his agents in positions of power or advising world leaders. He has gained control of military forces worldwide and has amassed various weapons, including nuclear arsenals, intending to challenge the gods. While most of the exiled ancient gods reside in the higher astral plane while awaiting judgment, Satan and a few of his followers constantly traverse between the astral plane and the physical world, assuming the bodies of their devotees through a form of demonic possession. Satan possesses a permanent body, while the demons are limited to temporary possessions. Regrettably, the only one available to aid us is Koka, who was renamed Kokabiel by the Creator, signifying star of God."

Luke, the historian, exclaimed, "Wow, that's incredible!" The rest of the team readily concurred and expressed their astonishment.

James weighed in. "Well, we certainly have our work cut out for us," and the team agreed. Thomas concluded, "Our mission must continue. All of you are absolutely right. We now comprehend the vastness and power of OWO, and we understand that the path ahead will not be easy. However, we must persevere; the fate of the world hangs in the balance." Ashlee and Joe proceeded to board the plane. They were resolved to continue their journey to Flagstaff.

CHAPTER EIGHTEEN

THE SACRED TABLET

A shlee and Joe woke up just as the flight attendant approached
and said, "We have arrived at Grand Canyon Pulliam Field, also
known as Flagstaff Pulliam Airport." They thanked her.

James's voice came up soon after. "Good morning. I hope you're
rested because you're in for a long day."

"We're good," Ashlee answered, throwing Joe a soft smile. He
squeezed her hand in return.

"Good," James stated before resuming. "Let me go over the details
of your mission."

"Go ahead; we're all ears," Joe replied.

James said, "We have a 2023, graphite-gray, four-wheel-drive Jeep
Renegade Latitude 4D sport utility vehicle waiting at the airport for
you. It will be in constant contact with Mia; she will program your
navigational system."

"I've already done it, and it's ready to go," Mia stated.

"Thank you, Mia," James said. "Afterward, you will drive to the
target area. Mia has programmed the coordinates you provided, and
it'll get you to the exact location. In the vehicle, you'll find a backpack
with some water, energy bars, and other items that may be useful for
your mission. And lastly, be careful. Our enemy agents will be tracking
you to try and stop you."

Ashlee nodded. "Don't worry; we'll get it done."

They exited the plane. It was a cloudy and rainy day with very

145

chilly temperatures. Ashlee spotted the Jeep and signaled to Joe, who followed her. They got in, started the engine, and drove off. Mia spoke up. "I have the navigational image projected to you both, and I'll keep you on the route to your destination. First, get on AZ-89A to I-17 North for 1.4 miles. Then take US-180 West to North Fort Valley Road to North Snow Bowl Road. It is a thirty-six-minute drive and, only 19.3 miles."

"OK." Joe nodded as he drove. "I'm very familiar with the area since I lived there for a few years."

Ashlee turned to look at Joe. "That's right, how did you like living in Sedona, and what brought you there?"

Joe grinned. "It was great! I enjoyed the outdoors. The weather was mild for the four seasons, and it's close to the airports in Flagstaff or Phoenix in case I wanted to go out of state. As to what brought me there, well, it all started when I was a child. I was always attracted to magic, mysticism, ancient stories, and books. I was fascinated by the stories in religious textbooks, having read by the time I was a teenager, the Bible, the Koran, and the teachings of Buddhism, Taoism, Confucius, and many others. I realized my mental awareness and inner energy increased as I acquired this knowledge.

"As a teenager, I learned meditation techniques and soon realized that it helped me build my energy, giving me a sensation of extreme well-being and power. Through meditation, I learned to focus my energy. At first, I learned to control my mental and bodily functions, and with time, I was able to project it to others and influence their behavior and actions. I realized that my energy was greater when my body and mind were in top shape, so I exercised daily and also practiced boxing and martial arts.

"As a child, I felt the need to help others, so I became a doctor. I enjoyed studying, and having a photographic mind made it easy for me to enter and graduate from medical school."

Ashlee chuckled and jokingly said, "Probably at the top of your class."

Joe smiled and said, "Yes. How did you know? Oh wait, you've been reading my thoughts. Anyway, after specializing in neurology, I joined and worked with a large medical group in New York. After years in a successful and highly lucrative private practice, during which I enjoyed a lavish lifestyle with a hectic social life, I felt it very unsatisfying and that something was missing. I never married. Since I turned forty, I have felt a strong urge to travel, so that's how I ended up in Sedona, teaching yoga and meditation."

Ashlee smiled at him before turning to stare out the window. "Well, that's great! Maybe someday—if we have one—we could settle down in Sedona."

Joe grinned wider, picked up her hand, and kissed the back of it. "I would love to, and hopefully, we would enjoy living there for the rest of our lives."

Ashlee blushed and squeezed his hand. "I would love that too."

Mia piped in just then. "We're approaching the right turn to North Snow Bowl Road. Take it and follow the road north until you reach the south parking lot on Road 516B. You'll find the entrance to Kachina Trail at the south end of this parking lot."

Joe steered the car to the given coordinates. "You got it. Is there anything suspicious in the area?"

"Not a thing. I have been monitoring for several miles around us, and everything seems OK," Mia said.

"Good." Ashlee sighed in relief, hoping this mission would be less intense than the rest. Once they arrived and parked, Joe took the backpack, and they proceeded to enter Kachina Trail.

At this point, Mia said, "Go south of this trail for approximately one mile until you reach a fairly large clearing in the forest."

"OK," Joe answered. They continued on the trail, which went through a dense forest. It seemed extraordinarily peaceful and serene, with no signs of anyone in the area. They walked about a mile, and as they approached the wide clearance in the forest, Joe asked, "What now, Mia?"

"For now, be alert; I detect seven human figures heading your way from the east and south of you."

"Great!" Ashlee rolled her eyes before throwing her hands up in frustration, "I thought you said it was clear."

Mia remained unaffected like the robot she was and answered airily, "It was at the time, but these just appeared a few seconds ago. They must have used a cloaking or jamming device to avoid detection."

Joe then projected a thought to Ashlee, "Are you ready?" Ashlee nodded in affirmation. At that point, the men appeared at the clearance and started firing on all cylinders by letting loose their ammo at them. Joe immediately created a colossal plasma ball and fired it at them, hitting three targets and stunning them. The rest were momentarily blinded, and Ashlee jumped into action, attacking the others. Joe joined her, and they went back and forth between them, attacking the remaining four enemy agents. They were using their martial arts' skills to attack and counterattack with fists, arms, and leg kicks. Their ability to read the enemy's thoughts and to anticipate their moves was helping.

But the agents that were stunned had recovered. Joe could see them ready to fire their weapons, but he knew he couldn't prevent it. From the corner of his eye, he saw twenty or so Native American men—based on how they were dressed—with badges and guns rushing toward them. They fired on the enemy agents, and an intense gun battle ensued. There were casualties on both sides, but finally, they were able to neutralize and subdue the enemy agents. Some of them were rendered unconscious. During this time, they could sense Koka assisting them by always making them aware of their and enemy agents' positions.

After defeating the enemy agents, Joe approached Ashlee and grabbed her waist as he absently checked for wounds. "Are you OK?"

"Never better," she answered as she smiled and wrapped her arms around his neck.

During that moment, they heard a voice behind them asking, "Hello, are you both OK?"

Ashlee flushed. Joe shook off the embarrassment and spoke up in as normal a tone as he could manage. "Yes, we are OK, thanks to you for giving us a hand, but who are you and what are you doing here?"

The apparent leader of the men said, "My name is Makya, which means hunting eagle in Hopi. I'm the chief or *kikmongwi* of my tribe, the Fire Clan." He then pointed to an elder standing beside him and said, "This is our *mongwi* or spiritual leader, who is responsible for the social and religious duties of the clan." Pointing at others, he said, "Those are our elders and some of our Hopi law-enforcement officers. So if you don't mind, we'll take those men who attacked you off your hands."

"Thank you," Ashlee said, finally recovering. "I'm very sorry you lost one of your officers, but I'm glad you were here to help us. How did you know we were here—not that I'm complaining?"

Pointing to his fallen officer, Makya said, "He was a good human and good warrior. He'll be with our ancestors telling them stories." All the men nodded in agreement. "We're here because our mongwi had a dream, during which, our Pahana, our lost white brother, appeared to him and told him to be at this location. He had returned, and he would need our help to assist you in everything you requested."

"I'm sorry," Ashlee slowly shook her head confusedly while Joe mirrored her expression, "but it's just us two. There's no one else with us."

The mongwi started speaking in his Ute Hopi dialect, and after he finished, he pointed at both Ashlee and Joe. "What did he say?" Joe asked.

Makya answered, "He said that our long-lost brother is living inside both of you and that he can communicate with him from the spirit world. Is this true?"

Ashlee exchanged a glance with Joe before answering. "It's a long story, but yes, we can merge our energies and bring him back into the astral plane or spirit world. That's why we're here. He told us about the sacred stone tablet of the Hopi Fire Clan and its location. We're supposed to retrieve it and use the information on it to save the earth."

The mongwi then signaled to proceed, so Joe asked Mia, "What's next?"

"A hundred and fifty feet to the west of that clearance is the location of the coordinates you provided. There seem to be some rock formations at that location. It might be an ancient lava ice cave. Hopefully, we'll find the sacred tablet in it," Mia supplied.

Ashlee and Joe walked to the rock formation. They were followed by the Hopi tribe. On the southern side, they located the entrance to the ice cave and proceeded to enter it. Once inside, they started looking for the tablet using their flashlights. The cave was approximately twenty by twenty feet in diameter.

Suddenly, the mongwi stopped them and started speaking in his dialect. "What did he say this time?" Joe inquired.

Makya replied, "You can't search any further until you show him the missing piece of the stone tablet that our lost white brother took with him." Ashlee and Joe looked at each other in confusion and said that they didn't have it.

The Hopi spiritual leader said something and pointed to the backpack. Joe said, "I believe he's telling us to look inside the backpack."

Up to that point, there had been no need to look inside of it. When Joe opened his backpack, he found a small gold metal box, and upon opening it, he saw a small piece of dark stone. He gave it to the mongwi. The mongwi then went to the east wall of the cave and pushed on a protruding rock.

Suddenly, the wall opened, and a two-foot-square space with a gold metal box appeared. When the Mongwi opened it, there was a dark stone tablet with a missing corner piece. The broken Hopi stone tablet was only four inches square and was given to the Hopi by Masaw, the deity of the Fire Clan. The mongwi took the piece Joe gave him and placed it in the missing area. It was a perfect fit, and immediately, as if by magic, the tablet became whole again. The Mongwi and the rest of the Hopi tribe started laughing and rejoicing. Then they exclaimed they welcomed back their long-lost white brother, whose return they had been waiting for, for many generations.

Ashlee and Joe were in awe and were speechless. Ashlee asked Mia, "Is this true? Is Koka the Pahana, the long-lost brother of the Hopi?"

"Yes," Mia confirmed, "before Kokabiel, he was known as Enki, Prometheus, Pahana, Quetzalcoatl, and by many other names. He helped create humankind. Once the decision had been made to destroy humankind, with mercy from the Most High, he managed to save the most righteous ones before the cataclysm. He taught them how to survive afterward. For thousands of years, he managed to pass on his DNA to humans. When the time came for his life cycle to end, he made his way back east to his outpost, Göbekli Tepe, promising to return one day."

The mongwi started narrating in his language while Makya translated. "There were four Hopi stone tablets of the Fire Clan. From ancient times, Masaw, the guardian of the underworld, gave these tablets to the Hopi, who requested that they keep them until several signs were fulfilled at the end of the fourth world and the beginning of the fifth world. When the warning signs occurred, the Hopi were instructed to reveal the tablets and their prophecies regarding the purification of the earth to the world. The Hopi tribe, seeing the warning signs in 1976, revealed the prophecies of the first three tablets to the world, but no one listened.

"The Hopi Fire Clan's dark stone tablet with the missing corner represents the final seal to be broken open at the end of the world to usher in a fifth-world paradise. This is the most important tablet. The only way to know the tablet's true and vital importance is by cracking open the tablet, which will reveal its information. Then the Hopi elders explore its significance. Such an act can only be performed when the missing piece is replaced in the corner. Otherwise, the tablet would simply crumble to dust. Thanks to you and our lost white brother, we were able to make it whole again.

"On December 21, 2012, a new era began, and it became the time to celebrate a coming together and the cycle of the Fire Clan. If we fast and pray in this cycle, purification will result, and we will be able to hear the humble voices of our ancestors or elders. These spirit elders offered the Hopi the tablets to assist in the purification process of the fourth world. We were told that when the lost white robed brother or Pahana returns, he would break open the Hopi's dark tablet and reveal its hidden, sacred teachings.

"It is said that the Creator desired to reveal the instructions of the great turning or shift of humanity into harmony with Mother Earth by those who were eager to listen. Massau had given them specific instructions to follow, which would assist in purifying the entire world after the fourth world had gone astray. Masaw gave the Hopi these tablets just before he turned his face from them and became invisible so that they would have a record of his words.

"This is what he said, as marked on the tablets: 'After the Fire Clan had migrated to their permanent home, the time would come when strange people would overcome them. They would be forced to develop their land and lives according to the dictates of a new ruler, or else, they would be treated as criminals and punished. But they were not to resist. They were to wait for the person who would deliver them. This person was their lost white brother, Pahana, who would return to them with the missing corner piece of the tablet. He would deliver them from their prosecutor overlords, who were yet to come, and work out a new and universal brotherhood of humankind with them.'"

"But Masaw warned that they must not accept any other religion (Baal worshipers), for this would be evil and would not save the people. On the stone tablets, the first three figures represent the first three worlds that have passed away. The fourth small human figure represents the fourth world where the Hopi have met the white man; this world, too, is passing away. The Hopi describe the large human figure on the left as the Great Spirit, with a bow in his left hand by the symbol of the churning earth and sun. Furthermore, the bow represents his instructions to the Hopi. The rod or line to the right of the Great Spirit represents a life path timeline.

"Yet the narrow path represents harmony with the earth and leads to a new world through a great trial and purification. After this purification, the cornstalk of a new abundance will grow when the Great Spirit returns. The tablets coincide with Hopi traditions and rituals, as described in their prophecy. They represent the Great Spirit as the purifier, the fourth world's coming to an end, and the symbol of corn as a return to harmony with the earth. We were told that the coming of Pahana would begin in the fifth world, and when all these signs are confirmed, there will be purification. So you see my white brother," he smiled and said while looking at Ashlee and Joe, "this is the ending of the fourth world and the beginning of the fifth world."

Joe turned toward Ashlee, who looked concerned, and exclaimed,

"Wow! You're telling us we have just fulfilled an ancient prophecy, and at the same time, we have triggered the end of times?"

Thomas spoke up, jolting both of them out of their thoughts. "Hi! Ashlee and Joe, we have been listening to everything, and it's incredible. We knew the dark piece of stone would come in handy, so we placed it in your backpack, which was retrieved from Göbekli Tepe. You both should know that the world's situation is rapidly deteriorating. We calculate that if nothing changes, the world will be at war or at least civil war by the end of the day. There will be total authority collapses in a majority of the countries. I believe it's time to have the world listen in and hear what we have discovered because it relates to the survival of all of us in the world."

"What do you mean by that?" Ashlee inquired.

"If we can put the Hopi elders and the mongwi on live TV and have them share with the world the information obtained as the tablet is split open by you and Joe, maybe we can help stop the chaos and madness going on everywhere," Thomas explained.

"That sounds like a great idea. What do we need to do to set it up?" Joe asked.

"Ask the tribal chief Makya if it's possible to use their facilities at Kykotsmovi, the seat of the Hopi's tribal government, which is located just below Third Mesa. Tell him that we have all the necessary audio-video broadcasting equipment to reach the world," Thomas instructed.

Joe turned toward Makya and relayed what Thomas had said. Makya talked to his elders and the mongwi and then told Joe, "Yes, we can go there and set it up. The mongwi told me that it is the duty of the Hopi tribe to share the prophecy with the world, including any new findings."

"Great! Let's go. Let's do it," Joe replied.

CHAPTER NINETEEN

WORLD CHAOS—SATAN

S atan saw that on the world stage, the situation had been rapidly deteriorating for several days. It was a result of years his agents of One World Order stepping up their efforts to achieve their goal of taking over the world and humanity. All of this was to confront and get revenge on the Most High, Yeshua, and his legions of angels. Satan, being the head of the OWO, had been plotting and planning this since he first took over the body of Tammuz, the son of Semiramis and Nimrod, thousands of years ago.

He had been in charge of the legions for the Most High until he was ousted after the rebellion and condemned to Earth and its surrounding astral planes. There, he was to remain until the end of times, awaiting his final judgment and fate. From the very start, he decided to take control of the world and use humans and their weapons, which he had a hand in helping develop. He also wanted to continue the battle that he had started in heaven, which he had no intention of losing.

He had managed to infiltrate and place his agents in all the world's governments. For instance, they had become the personal advisors to the heads of state or the persons in charge of the military and security forces. Using their high government positions, they provided terrible advice to the heads of state, or using their control of the armed forces, they initiated skirmishes with other countries. His agents had infiltrated every organization and protest movement all over the world, with the purpose of making sure that every movement became violent. He intended to cause the collapse civil authority and to create a state of anarchy. He had managed to get nations to go to war with one another or to threaten to do so and to have the majority of the countries on the verge of collapse from civil unrest.

He created an image of himself as a wealthy, successful businessman and philanthropist, who cared for humankind. The European community considered him to be someone with good judgment and wisdom. So taking advantage of the chaos, he offered his services to the European Union, promising to bring law and order to the European nations and mediation to the countries at war with one another.

The European Union was desperate and at a crossroads, not knowing how to stop the madness happening everywhere or which direction to take. So when this outstanding wealthy businessman and philanthropist offered his services, they were immensely relieved and grateful. He was well known to all of them, and they didn't hesitate to give him the power. At a meeting four weeks earlier, the president of the European Council nominated him for president of the European Commission. Immediately, the president of the European Parliament appointed him as president of the European Commission.

As the president of the European Commission, he now led the commission, executive, and cabinet of the European Union. Therefore, he held the most powerful position within the EU. As part of this institution, the president was responsible for European law's political direction, logistics, and implementation. The role allowed him to allocate portfolios to dismiss and reshuffle European commissioners and to direct the commission's civil service. The commission had representation offices throughout the EU, which acted as the commission's voice and monitored public opinion in their host country.

They also had 139 offices outside the EU, which were known as delegations. The European External Action Service managed them. They presented, explained, and carried out the EU's foreign policies as dictated by the president. They also analyzed policies, created reports, and negotiated for the EU. As president of the European Commission, his government office and headquarters were at the Rue de la Loi 200, 1040, Brussels, Belgium, which was located in Le Berlaymont near the Parc du Cinquantenaire. This was near his personal residence, where he had been living since the birth of his current body. With this, Satanail or as the European Union knew him, Mr. Seth Devlin—well-dressed in a three-piece suit, middle-aged, physically fit businessman with a well-trimmed mustache and goatee—had become the most influential person in Europe.

He was now in a position to control and direct the European nations and affect the outcome of world affairs. His identity was only known by Charles, his loyal servant and right-hand man, and the high council of his One World Order secret society.

They were in his government office when Charles asked, "What's our next move, my lord? We have everyone in place and waiting to carry out your orders in every country worldwide."

Satan smiled cruelly, leaning back in his seat. "Great! Tonight at midnight, I will give orders to all armed forces to attack one another with the pretext that they are defending themselves from aggressors. At the same time, you will order all our agents to riot, destroy, and kill wherever they are. We will topple the civil authorities to create anarchy and mayhem. By the end of the day tomorrow, I want to take control of the earth because soon, we will be confronting my father and his legions, so we need to be ready."

Charles bowed. "Yes, my lord. It will be as you command." With this, what had been predicted and seen in Revelation 17 happened: a crisis so significant that a core group of leaders will cede authority to a central power as the only solution for the stability for world order. This power would emerge differently than we see today, yet it would be firmly rooted in ancient and medieval tradition. It would offer what seemed to be the only viable hope of human survival and prosperity.

CHAPTER TWENTY

THE VOICE

Thomas was in the underground headquarters of the Group with the rest of the team. They had monitored Ashlee and Joe during their mission to San Francisco Mountain. The OWO agents had just been defeated, and Ashlee and Joe were talking to the Hopi natives. Plus, everyone had just agreed to meet at the facilities at Kykotsmovi.

Suddenly, Thomas got a call from their benefactor and hurried to the secured conference room to take it. Thomas answered, "Yes, sir, I'm here."

The voice said, "I'm going to put you and Joe on a three-way conference call for now. Joe will listen to our conversation while driving to the meeting place on the Hopi reservation." The voice added Joe. "Joe, I've been communicating with Thomas for many years. A group of super-wealthy people, including myself, have been funding the Group in its fight against the evil One World Order."

Surprised, Joe replied, "Hi! Nice speaking to you. Is there a problem?"

"No," he said, "I just want to give you some information you need to know. I founded the Group many years ago after being approached by a man, only known as Charles of One World Order, inviting me to join them. He stated that he was the personal representative of the leader of their secret society and that he had the authority to invite me into the society and answer all of my questions. I had just taken control of our family business and was looking forward to running it and improving it if possible.

"Charles explained to me that for security reasons, he could not disclose the name of his leader, whom he referred to as his lord. He stated that only he and the high council of their secret society knew his identity. He told me of their organizational structure and that I would be in charge of the local cell in New York, where I was living.

"When he informed me of their purpose, I first thought he was joking and told him I was not amused by it. He assured me that he was not joking and was earnest because their purpose was to take over control of the earth—the entire planet—to create one government and one army, all controlled by one leader, his lord. I told him that he was delusional and that it was impossible and crazy. Very seriously, he replied that they had been preparing for this for thousands of years and that they had followers in all the governments, armed forces, businesses, societies, universities, protest groups, and popular movements worldwide just waiting for the order to act. They were in a position to create chaos, start wars among the countries, and destabilize governments to weaken those authorities, which would make it easy for them to take control of the world.

"I made it evident that I believed he was exaggerating the extent and control of his ancient secret society, so he asked me to pick a city in any part of the world. To go along with it, I said Madrid. He used his cell phone and said to whoever was on the other end, 'Madrid.' He then turned to me and asked me to turn on world news and to pay attention to anything regarding Madrid. He stated that they would be reporting an explosion from a suicide bomber on the grounds of the Madrid Royal Palace.

A short while later, world news interrupted their regular broadcast to report that an explosion had been reported from the Madrid Royal Palace a few minutes earlier. They were still assessing the situation, but apparently, it had been a suicide bomber. I couldn't believe what I had just heard. I realized right there and then that this One World Order secret society was evil and very dangerous to the world. I asked Charles to leave my office immediately and never to return, saying that I would never join such a group of evil people. He grinned and suddenly looked very menacing, and without saying anything else, he left. I not only rejected their evil scheme but also decided to stop them. This made me an instant target, and assassins were immediately sent to eliminate me. Up to this point, I had been a businessman in the banking industry, which had made me very wealthy."

"OK," said Joe. "That's very interesting, and we know they are very evil, but why are you telling me all this?"

"Well, you see," he continued, "all that changed when I met a beautiful woman during one of my business trips to Phoenix, Arizona. She was an art critic and very well known in that circle. We were at a charity gala event when I saw her there, and it was love at first sight. After dating, I asked her to marry me, and she said yes. I married a beautiful woman who gave me a wonderful son, whom I adored. We lived in a New York mansion and had staff members who cared for our needs. I would go to work every day, and my wife, Sarah, would stay home and care for our son. She had put her career as an art critic on hold to raise our son. We loved spending all our free time together as a family, which I used to believe would last forever. I had the perfect family and life until one dreadful day.

I was driving my family to our country estate for a bit of family time when we were attacked on the road. Our vehicle was hit by a missile, which was fired from a helicopter. It overturned our car, making it burst into flames. I was able to make it out of the car with my son. After I put him down a safe distance from the car, I rushed back to get my wife, but at that moment, it exploded. Just like that, she was gone, and I fell on my knees and cried for the longest time until I heard my son crying. At that moment, I decided that my wife's death would not be in vain and that I would dedicate all my resources to fighting back and stopping the OWO. I would fight back and not let this evil prevail, but first, I had to make sure my son was safe and taken care of. I made the difficult decision to have my son adopted by a couple who would love and raise him in a loving family environment. It was a deliberate attempt to keep him safe and away from me, which would put him in harm's way. I ensured that all his and his new family's needs would always be addressed.

"I watched him grow into a fine, handsome man and good person. I was very proud when he became a doctor because I knew he would help humankind. Yes, Joe, I'm your father. I'm so sorry that you didn't know your mother and that I couldn't keep you at my side. I didn't want you to discover your origins like this, but circumstances dictated it."

There was complete silence. Joe felt a warm hand encompass his own, and he turned to see the love and concern in the eyes of the woman he had begun to love. It gave him strength that he did not know he had. He smiled at her before turning back to the windshield. "I understand. I know it had to have been a difficult decision for you." He met Ashlee's eyes again and spoke softly. "I finally know what love is and can relate to all of this." She smiled at him.

The voice said, "Your mother came from a long line of mystic women. The day you were born, she told me that you were special and that you had a mission in life, which was going to help humankind. I see now what she was referring to, and I will ensure you have everything you need to accomplish it. I have been living with an assumed identity—Gabriel Powers—in a downtown apartment. From there, I have been coordinating our resources to fight OWO. But my real name is Joshua Alexander, which is also your last name, Joe."

"Wow!" Thomas exclaimed. Shock and excitement were palpable in his voice. "Are you the Alexander of Alexander Banking Corporation, the biggest bank in the world?"

"Yes," he replied. "Now that you are in harm's way, Joe, it doesn't matter that they know I'm still alive and have a son. I'm getting old, and I don't have the energy that I used to, so you, being my only heir, have replaced me as the president of the Alexander Banking Corporation as of today. My lawyers will contact you at some point. You will assume total control, and you can direct the resources you need to the Group. Thomas will continue to be the director of the Group and will follow your orders from here on in. I hope to meet you in person and maybe spend some time with you, but we will see what happens after you break the fourth sacred tablet. Take care, and

Thomas, you have been loyal to me and the Group. Please continue in the same way with my son."

"Yes, sir, don't worry. I will always look after him," Thomas replied solemnly.

Joe remained silent before a small smile curved on his lips, and tears rolled down his face. "I, too, hope there's time someday to get to know each other, Father. And maybe you can tell me more about my mother." He couldn't see or hear his father, but something told him that he was smiling too. The thought gave him unexpected peace.

CHAPTER TWENTY-ONE

THE RETURN

Ashlee and Joe arrived at the Hopi government tribal facilities at Kykotsmovi. Makya, the elders, and many other people were already waiting there. They approached the Group and asked who else was there. Makya stood up and gestured to a group of men. "These are our leaders, the Hopi tribal council—our chairman, vice-chairman, secretary, treasurer, and sergeant at arms. They have been briefed, and they welcome you to our town. In the main chamber where the council holds their meetings, your team is setting up all the equipment Thomas sent here."

Peter's voice sounded through the ear coms. "Hey, guys, I'm in the main chamber setting up all our electronic equipment. We should be able to live broadcast in approximately one hour, and with Mary's help, we will be able to interrupt all the stations around the globe and insert our signal and broadcast."

"That's right," Mary confirmed. "I will have you on every private and government monitor worldwide. It is a onetime shot, and we will have about twenty to thirty minutes before we get cut off by our enemy, One World Order."

"Thank you, Mary," replied Ashlee. "We'll make it count."

Joe turned to Makya and said, "Once we have the audio video up and running, we'll broadcast live to the whole world. As the translator, you and your mongwi spiritual leader will face the camera. Knowing that the world is watching, tell it what you have been trying to warn humankind about for many years. We don't have much time, so make it count."

Makya bowed. "Thank you both for allowing us once more to try and get our message out. With this, we will have fulfilled our mission to warn the world of what's to come. If the world doesn't listen, I guess I don't have to worry about a TV career." He chuckled. Joe and Ashlee laughed.

Ashlee said, "I hope they do listen. But if after you speak to them, they don't want to change, Joe and I will split open the dark sacred tablet in front of the whole world. Then we'll see what follows."

Peter interrupted them, saying, "OK, everyone, I'm ready. Do you want to join me in the main chamber?"

"Great!" Joe answered, "We'll be right in." They all went to the main chamber, where they saw the broadcasting equipment set up and a small, elevated stage with the background of an American eagle in flight on the wall.

Peter said, "Makya, could you and your mongwi stand up there on the stage with Ashlee and Joe standing behind you?"

"Sure," he replied. They all took their positions.

Peter smiled, gave them a thumbs-up, and said, "I will count to three, and then you'll be live, so you can start talking." He said, "One, two, three." Then he pointed to Makya.

Makya said, "Hello, world, we have interrupted your signal to bring you this critically special message. It is being broadcast on every channel in every country across the globe. My name is Makya; I'm the chief, *kikmongwi*, of the Fire Clan and a member of the Hopi Independent Nation. I have been asked to translate for our spiritual leader and elders of the Hopi people. We are here to fulfill our clan's duty by presenting to all the nations of the world, the message that the Great Spirit entrusted to us thousands of years ago in our sacred stone tablets.

"But first, I would like to remind the world of a Hopi spiritual leader, who in 1976, stood in front of the United Nations Habitat Forum in Vancouver, British Columbia, and delivered a warning message for humankind because of the destruction of land and life that was taking place. He wanted humanity to know that the end-of-time warning signs were happening but that they had a chance to change the direction of that movement, to do a roundabout turn, and to move in the direction of peace, harmony, and respect for land and life. He wanted everyone to know that the time was right back then and that later would be too late. In order to do that, the people had to return to the spiritual path as one to cure and heal Mother Earth. Only through the heart, prayer, and ceremony can we halt this turbulence of evil. Unfortunately, no one listens, and now, here we are delivering not a warning but a final prophecy to all humankind."

Makya took a deep breath. His eyes were grave, his expression was somber, and he continued speaking. "Hopi spiritual leaders are greatly concerned with the conditions of our Mother Earth. They have watched the systematic destruction of people and natural resources. According to our beliefs and prophecies, humankind's existence will soon end if this destruction continues. According to Hopi prophecy, we are simply trying to inform the world of what is going to happen if the destruction of the earth and its people continue, as it is known by our religious Hopi elders.

"The land was here long before any human being set foot upon this earth. The human race began somewhere, and we came to this land after asking permission from the Great Spirit through Massau. After obtaining his approval, we arrived and settled on this land. He showed us the continent and gave us sacred stone tablets, religious instructions, warnings, and prophecies. Hence, all land and life were placed in the care of Kikmongwis and religious headmen. He marked out the boundaries for each group on each continent, after which each group was given an individualized life plan with specific spiritual and religious beliefs—the way to worship and live, the food to eat, the languages to speak, and the like.

"He then gave his final instructions: 'Live and never lose faith or turn away from your life pattern.' The people of the world are turning away from their life plans. We Hopi have been faithful to the instructions of the Great Spirit through Massau up to this time. We have followed our life plan, are still holding on to our sacred rights and ceremonies, and have not lost our faith. He has given us many prophecies and told us the white brother would come and be a brilliant man, bringing to us many things he would invent.

"Massau said that a time will come when a gourd of ashes will be dropped upon the earth, and many men will die, which will mark the end of the materialistic way of life. We do not want to see this happen again in any place on Mother Earth. Instead, we should use all this energy for peaceful things and not wage war. Today, the sacred lands where the Hopi live are being desecrated by people who seek coal, minerals, and water from our soil so that they may create more power for the white brother's cities. It will destroy the Hopi and other people with smog, poison air, and cause a lack of water and pollution of water and land.

"Sacred Hopi land is in ruins all over the Four Corners area, where Arizona, New Mexico, Colorado, and Utah meet in the United States. Hopis called this area Tukunavi, which is part of Mother Earth's heart. It has been a shrine and sacred place for the Hopi and other pueblos for many thousands of years. This desecration of our spiritual center must not be allowed to continue, for if it does, Mother Nature will react in such a way that almost all people will suffer the end of life as they now know it.

"All we ask is that this place be respected and protected by all nations, who have a sacred duty and responsibility to take every measure to preserve this spiritual center. Massau said not to take from the earth for destructive purposes and not to destroy living things indiscriminately or without prayer. He further stated that humankind was to live in harmony and maintain a good, clean land for all children so that they could come and take care of the land and life for the Great Spirit. The nations of the world have gone against these instructions, and now, they have almost destroyed all our land and way of life.

"The Hopi people and other first people are standing on this religious principle to care for and maintain the earth and our existence. It is the need of the hour. The United States and the United Nations should understand that they cannot bring about peace, harmony, or the good life in the world without correcting the wrongdoings that are going on. From now on, people must learn to serve others and to share freely. We must bring back the level of life where land and water are free, there are no boundaries, and there is freedom of spiritual understanding."

The mongwi then started speaking in his language, and after he finished, Makya began to translate. "Our mongwi spiritual leader said that we want to share some prophecy from the Hopi nation, specifically the Hopi prophecy of Joseph White Eagle. The Hopis' ancient knowledge and prophecies are warning signs, which we are seeing nowadays. They tell us that we have entered a dangerous period in our lives. Humankind must return to peaceful ways and halt the destruction of Mother Earth, or else we will completely decimate ourselves.

"All the stages of Hopi prophecy have come to pass, except for the last purification process. The intensity of this purification will depend on how humanity collaborates with the Creator. We are entering the last days, and we must correct and change our ways, return to spiritual practices, and take care of Mother Earth. If we do not, we will face terrible destruction by nature, bringing purification or destruction. The more we turn away from the instructions of the Great Spirit, the more signs we see in the form of earthquakes, floods, drought, fires, tornadoes, wars, and corruption.

"Because of the Hopis' deep spiritual qualities and sensitivity to nature, we know that the essential electromagnetic balance of life forces is maintained through nature's gifts of minerals, water, sunlight, atmospheric currents, charged ion fields, sacred rituals, and ceremonial dances. Reverence for life is a protection for all the people of the earth, for we are all bound together in a global grid pattern of energy. Another Hopi prophecy has come to pass. We were told that when the lost white robed brother or Pahana returns, he would break open the Hopi dark sacred tablet and reveal its hidden holy teachings.

"It is said that the Creator desired to reveal the instructions of the great turning or the shift of humanity into harmony with Mother Earth to those who were eager to listen. Massau had given us specific instructions to follow that would assist in purifying the entire world after the fourth world had gone astray. We were also told that the coming of our lost white brother would usher in the ending of the fourth world and the beginning of the fifth world, and when all these signs are confirmed, there will be purification."

Then turning and pointing to Ashlee and Joe, Makya said, "Here you see my white brother." Looking toward Ashlee and Joe, he said, "They are sharing their bodies and living in both of them. Our Pahana is the only one capable of breaking the tablet without it crumbling into dust." Makya and the mongwi moved aside, and Ashlee and Joe stepped forward into the spotlight.

Ashlee held up the dark, sacred stone tablet, which was now whole and intact. She said, "A being many thousands of years old lives in both of us," as she pointed to Joe. "He identified himself as Kokabiel, who is also known as Enki, Prometheus, Pahana, Quetzalcoatl, and many others. He has the power to split open the final sacred tablet we're holding. Doing so will signal the end of this fourth world and usher in the beginning of the new fifth world. But if you are willing to change and return to peaceful ways, correct and change your ways, go back to the spiritual ways, and halt the destruction of Mother Earth, we will not break open the sacred tablet. The intensity of the purification will depend on how humanity collaborates with the Creator. But we are entering the end of days. If we do not change, we are going to face terrible destruction by nature, bringing purification or destruction."

Joe added, "My associate will permit you to broadcast so that we can view the replies of all the nations in the world. Be aware that agents of an ancient secret society—One World Order—have infiltrated all the world governments, societies, organizations, and armies. They want the world's destruction so they can take it over and use us to battle our Creator, Jesus, the prophets, and the legions of angels that are coming with him. Their leader is Satan, who by now must be in a powerful position because he probably promised you that he could solve the chaos afflicting the world. But he can't; all he'll accomplish is bringing the wrath of God upon us. You can identify their agents by their advice or actions, which are always to fight and attack or no peace, compromise, or dialogue. So if you have these persons next to you, they are not your friends but your enemies."

Peter had set up huge monitors with multiple windows. At this point, they displayed many leaders, who had their advisors and generals next to them, and showed the anger and chaos reigning in most of the nation's broadcasting and the yelling at and questioning of who they thought they were to dictate what to do. They asked them to show proof of what was being said and to stop holding their broadcasting stations hostage. They further stated that they had to protect themselves from aggressive nations, questioning how they could consider peace when threatened by others. It was evident that the message didn't get through to them.

Ashlee and Joe then raised their arms, and while holding the dark sacred stone tablet, they each pulled on it, slitting it in two halves like a book. They showed it to the mongwi, who read its symbols and started speaking in his language. When he stopped, Makya said, "Our mongwi spiritual leader says that the tablet is announcing that the Great Spirit and Yeshua are coming to Earth with an army of angels for judgment day."

At this point—abruptly—all over the world, hundreds and maybe thousands of shiny silver-and-gold-colored spheres appeared in the sky over all the cities and population centers of every nation, country, and continent. And then they emitted a deafening noise that sounded like a trumpet; it was heard in every corner building and basement worldwide. The monitors went silent, and heads of state could be seen startled and amazed at what was happening.

After a few minutes, the trumpets stopped, but the spheres remained in place. The mongwi said something else, and when he stopped, Makya began speaking again, "The mongwi said these spheres are the watchers for the Great Spirit. They have been here since the beginning. They will remain until the arrival of the Great Spirit, and they want to remind us that the intensity of the purification will depend on how humanity collaborates with the Creator."

At this point, one could see, on the many monitors, the heads of state ordering the removal of what seemed to be advisors, generals, and the like. One could hear them pledging to follow the path of peace and return to the spiritual path. Ashlee and Joe hugged each other, and just like the Group, they also observed what was happening on the monitors. They couldn't help thinking that maybe humankind and Mother Earth had just gotten a second chance.

Suddenly, one could hear various global broadcasting stations excitedly repeating the same message over the monitors and speakers. "An enormous object over a hundred miles in diameter had just been spotted entering our solar system."

Joe turned to Ashlee and while holding her hand, said, "Listen, there is a dead silence from everyone in the world."

After the initial silence, some leaders, especially in Europe, could be heard saying, "Now's the time for all mankind to unite and fight back; we have to defend ourselves." Then all the monitors went dead.

The mongwi, the Hopi spiritual leader, said, "The breaking of the last sacred tablet seal is announcing the end of our world and the return of the Great Spirit for final judgment. The spheres will continue watching us until the arrival of the Creator and will sound warnings of impending punishment and destruction if humanity continues to ignore our covenant with him."

Joe looked at Ashlee, and she nodded. Then he said, "Thomas, we have to regroup and plan our next move. This battle against evil is just beginning."

"Yes," he replied, "we'll meet at headquarters. Hopefully, we can prevent the sounding of more trumpets by the watchers and the unleashing of hell on earth."

Joe turned to look at the Hopi leaders and the mongwi spiritual guide and said, "Thank you for helping us; I just hope that humankind can survive what's coming."

CHAPTER TWENTY-TWO

REGROUP

Ashlee, Joe, and the rest of the Group's members gathered all their equipment and boarded helicopters, which were waiting to take them to the Flagstaff airport for their flight back to New York. The stations worldwide were broadcasting the same message very excitingly. "An enormous object over a hundred miles in diameter has just been spotted entering our solar system."

After the initial dead silence from everyone in the world, some leaders, especially in Europe, could be heard broadcasting and saying, "Now's the time for all humankind to unite and fight back; we have to defend ourselves. You don't want to be slaves or servants."

During the flight back to New York, Ashley reflected on and pondered humanity's future. She could sense that Joe was thinking and concerned also about his future with her and the world. They were still in awe from witnessing the spheres and sound of what seemed to be a trumpet. More important was that they had probably triggered the beginning of the end for their world. Of course, they didn't know it, but it would have had the same result if they had broken the seal or not. One World Order would have unleashed worldwide chaos, war, and the toppling of governments if the spheres had not appeared.

Many governments and countries worldwide have decided to change their ways, promising to follow a more righteous path with peace and goodwill for all. Also, they would respect Mother Earth and not abuse or cause destruction. Because of the breaking of the sacred tablet, humankind had been warned, and if it didn't change its ways, there would be a severe purification, which meant elimination. This could be from further disasters triggered by the trumpet's sound or by the Creator upon his return, which they now knew was happening.

They finally arrived at headquarters, and almost immediately, Mia came on the coms, saying, "There's a meeting for all team members at command center in twenty minutes." Ashlee and Joe went to their respective apartments, agreeing to meet at the command center.

When Ashlee arrived at the center, everyone else was already there. There was a very somber feel to it. Everyone looked worried and even a bit scared. After the greetings were over, Thomas said, "We're still assessing the situation; a lot has happened in the past twenty-our hours. First, let me review what we know. We now know that the ancient gods and the Creator are real. There seems to be a consensus among us that there's probably going to be a judgment of humankind. We still don't know if this is going to be a good or bad thing. We must assume that resistance is futile against an entity who is capable of interstellar travel and probably highly advanced. Our most viable alternative is not to show hostility but to show a willingness to change our ways and follow its recommendations for a more righteous path. Maybe this is an opportunity to benefit from an advanced species and their technology for the good of mankind. We don't stand a chance if they decide to terminate us, and it's fairly clear that will happen if we don't follow the covenant presented to us."

Mary added, "I have been monitoring the TV and radio stations around the world. It seems that most of the governments and countries in North, Central, and South America are choosing to follow the covenant with the Creator. They have removed anyone who favored war or violent measures and have replaced them with peace-loving persons. In Europe, we have a split, with approximately ten countries calling for people to take up arms and fight back what they are calling an alien invasion and promising to use nuclear weapons to defend themselves. In Africa and Asia, there are many countries ready to follow the call to arms from the president of the European Commission, but as of now, they are still undecided."

Mia said, "With Peter's help, I have been monitoring communications worldwide, and it seems to be highly concentrated in the Belgium region. This could be a coincidence because many of the important European high offices are in this area, or it could be where the orders to the dissenting countries originate from."

"Thank you, Mia. Does anyone else have something to say?"

The history expert Luke said, "I'm still in shock; I never dreamed that the gods of our ancient civilizations were going to return and that we would be face-to-face with them. From written history, humankind never fares well after challenging the gods. As Thomas has pointed out, I would advise that we not show hostility, which means we must convince the rest of the world to do the same. I doubt that the gods will make a distinction based on borders. I believe we'll all be in it together, good or bad."

Mathew the religious expert added, "Also, we should keep in mind that in all the cultures and religions around the world, anytime humans repented and asked for mercy, it seemed to have been granted by a god or the gods. We have no reason to believe the contrary in this situation. Of course, if a segment of our population initiates a war, who knows what will happen to us?

James said, "There's a lot of work to be done. We know that One World Order is behind the call to arms. We need to stop it and figure out how to convince the gods of our good intentions."

Thomas asked, "Ashlee and Joe, you have been quiet. Is there anything you would like to say?"

Ashlee looked at Joe and then answered, "I'm still trying to wrap my head around everything that has happened. Just a few months ago, my most significant decision was what to have for dinner. Now, I'm not sure if I'll be around to eat dinner a few months from now. But I do know that we have to try and survive for the good of humanity."

Joe nodded and said, "I agree with Ashlee; we have to try to do the best we can to survive."

"OK," said Thomas, "as of this moment, we will put all our efforts into stopping One World Order. And the best way to do this is to cut the head off the snake. That means we will not only fight them in each country or entity where they are embedded but also give priority to localizing their headquarters and eliminating their leaders. I have to go to the United Nations' headquarters, where emergency meetings occur. I will be briefing them on what we are up against and how to fight it since the world's fate is at stake. Everyone knows what to do until I return in a few days. Take care team and also get some rest. You deserve it." Everyone wished him well as he was leaving.

Ashlee and Joe retired to their quarters. They held hands and looked into each other's eyes. They wished each other goodnight, although they wanted to stay together and continue holding each other.

Joe went into his apartment and straight to his bedroom. He was lying on the bed, staring at the ceiling, and thinking how complicated his life had gotten suddenly. He wasn't concerned with his future fate; he figured he had had a good life and had done the best that he could. But he was feeling sad because he didn't know if he would spend the rest of his life with Ashlee, the wonderful woman he had met and fallen in love with. He was more afraid for her and what her future might hold. Joe decided that he would take a shower and try to get some rest.

Joe had just finished showering, and he was ready to go to bed when there was a knock on his door. Mia asked, "Ashlee is at the door. Do you want me to let her in?"

Joe replied, "Yes, immediately. Then could you disconnect and give us some privacy, please?"

Mia answered, "No problem. Call me if you need me."

As soon as the door opened, Joe was there to greet Ashlee, saying, "Hi! Is everything OK? Is anything wrong?"

Ashlee smiled and said, "Yes, don't worry, everything is fine. Well, not really. I feel a little confused and scared. I just don't want to be alone, and the thought of not being with you in the future was agonizing for me. I don't know what the future holds for us, but at this moment, I want to be with you."

With this, Joe put his arms around her waist and pulling her toward him, said, "There's nothing more important in my life than being with you. I don't know what's in store for us, but tonight, nothing else exists except us." With this, they embraced for a long time. Mia closed the door and turned the lights off.

AUTHOR'S NOTE

In my lifetime, I have seen the technological advances that humankind has achieved and the amazing miracles that we can perform, such as flying ships, space exploration, medical advances to prolong life and resuscitation, etc. We have gradually moved away from our religious beliefs toward scientific proof to explain the unknown. I, like millions of other people in this world, have had questions regarding our origin. Did we evolve naturally, or were we created? Were we created by God? Are the stories and myths of ancient gods true? Are we alone in the universe? What's our purpose in life? What's humankind's future and fate?

Since childhood, I have read everything I could to answer these questions but have never found satisfactory answers. I decided to combine all these elements and formulate a plausible explanation for everything we have always wondered about. I'm not a writer, but I attempted to create a fictitious narrative of my interpretation and make it entertaining at the same time. I hope you enjoyed reading this novel as much as I enjoyed writing it.

ABOUT THE AUTHOR

Jose has loved reading since childhood and has been interested in the metaphysical, including science fiction, ancient civilizations, the Bible, world religions, and mysticism. He went to medical school and practiced for nearly forty years. He lives in Arizona with his partner and enjoys travel around the world. This is his first book.

ANUNNAKI

Made in the USA
Las Vegas, NV
22 October 2024

10323379R00121